Same time next year?

Ships don't always pass in the night

J M Hampshire

Halfwaytree Publishing

Acknowledgments:
I owe a huge debt of thanks to the following team of people, all of whom have had crucial roles in the compilation and publishing of this book.

Alpha reader: My Alpha reader is my beautiful wife, who quite simply has more faith in me than I do, but who also has an incredible eye for detail, and whose advice and insight is my inspiration to keep writing.

Beta readers: To my Beta readers, Judith Prescott and Rychard Winslade; thank you both for your time, dedication and honesty – you have the final say on the story line and characters, and I am so grateful for your help and support.

Editor: The manuscript has been beautifully edited and polished by Lee Ellwood of EllWords Editing and Writing, whom I cannot recommend highly enough (https://ellwords.com.au).

Cover design by Ashley Santoro

Interior formatting / typesetting by Atticus

An imprint of Halfwaytree Publishing Pty Ltd

ISBN:
978-0-6454399-6-0 (Paperback)
978-0-6454399-1-5 (Hardback)
978-0-6454399-2-2 (ebook)

First published in 2022
Third edition 2022

Email: jm@jmhampshire.com
Website: www.jmhampshire.com

A catalogue record for this book is available from the National Library of Australia.

A number of doggies were thoroughly spoiled during the writing of this book.

For my wonderful wife.
Without whose help,
support, belief in me,
and attention to detail,
this book simply wouldn't exist.

FaB-Ex '91

1

'For Chrissake, stop looking at the skirt and pay attention to what you're doing!'

'Sorry, Chilly,' Jamie replied sheepishly, but his supervisor wasn't quite finished.

'Jesus, maybe I should have worn a bloody skirt, then perhaps you might listen to me instead of eyeing up the local talent all the time.'

Again, 'Sorry, Chilly.' Jamie took a deep breath and tried to commit to the task in front of him. He needed this job.

He was aware of giggling from off to his right and knew he was being watched but steeled himself not to look. His supervisor, Len Winterbottom, would only take so much and Jamie could see he was close to breaking point. They had two installations to complete in the day, and delays with the services had meant that they were already behind schedule.

For obvious reasons, Len had earned the nickname 'Chilly-Arse', which was then shortened to 'Chilly' by his workmates and which he seemed quite comfortable with. It was probably better than some of the names the other installation engineers were called.

Jamie felt himself drifting off again and forced himself to concentrate. He was holding the foot and leg of a large piece of process equipment aligned and together while Chilly tightened the securing bolts.

'Do each one up finger tight first,' Chilly instructed, 'then go round and check they're all in the right position and not rucking up the carpet. Then go round them all again and tighten them up.' Jamie liked Chilly; he acted gruff, but he was a big-hearted man and a good mentor.

He heard another giggle from his right, coming from the four girls on the stand opposite. *Oh, please don't let Chilly's arse crack be on show*, he thought. Chilly had a habit of not pulling his trousers up properly, and when he bent over—which in this profession was frequently—his white Y-fronts and the cleft of his buttocks would make a guest appearance. Jamie tried not to smirk at the image in his mind, but his face must have registered some amusement.

'Oh, I'm sorry,' Chilly reprimanded, 'is something funny?'

'No, no, not at all, Chilly,' Jamie stammered. 'Just getting cramp in my thigh,' he lied.

Chilly shook his head, and the two of them moved on to the next leg. Jamie was pleased to see him hoist his trousers up as they moved round. From this, the final leg, he could see the four girls on the stand opposite. He had heard them laughing as they walked towards the stand a few minutes earlier. With no carpet down yet along the walkways, their high heels had clicked noisily, and his well-tuned young male ear had picked up the sound from a long way away.

He had watched them approaching as Chilly rattled on about the difference between coarse and fine threads. Each girl had a takeaway coffee and was laughing openly; they all looked so happy and carefree that Jamie found himself smiling at them. All four were dressed in some kind of uniform, with a logo and company name emblazoned across their tight shirts above short, bright-red skirts. They looked very much like American college cheerleaders and the bright colours very out of place in this dirty environment.

Both the skirts and shirts were very revealing. The V necklines were low cut, showing cleavage, and the skirts barely covered their dignity. They had obviously been designed – and the girls chosen – to entice the male contingent at the show onto their stand. Jamie looked up at the stand above them; the main signage told him the company name was 'Wow!' then, in smaller letters, said 'for all your catering needs'. With a company name like that, it was no wonder they had decided to go with models as front-of-house. He looked back at the four girls, only one of whom was now facing him, and could see the 'Wow!' logo on the shirt across her chest, with 'for all your catering needs' in smaller lettering underneath. In fact the word 'catering' was very small, and he had to squint to see it clearly.

The girl noticed Jamie peering at her shirt, and to his horror she tugged it downwards with her free hand so that he could read it. The other three girls saw her gesture and looked to see who it was for. There was no escape; he had been caught staring. He had genuinely been trying to read the wording, nothing more, but he guessed that wasn't how it looked. He smiled back at her, the smile of someone caught in the act—part guilt, part courtesy. He pointedly turned away to watch what Chilly was doing. Thankfully, the older man's face was pressed against the cold stainless steel, looking in the opposite direction, and he hadn't seen this interaction across the walkway.

'How's it going, Chilly?' Jamie asked, to try to close off the incident. In the background he heard the girls laughing, and it took all his willpower not to look back at them.

'Yep, that's it,' Chilly confirmed. He put the spanner down on the carpet next to the foot and took a deep breath. 'Time for a cup of tea, I think, don't you?'

'What about the compressed air?' Jamie wanted to keep the conversation going, aware that the four girls were trying to distract him, but he purposely didn't look. Surely they would lose interest in him soon.

'Doesn't look like they're in a rush to come and fit it, does it? So we'll have a cuppa and go start the other job, then come back to this one later. It's in the next hall.'

Jamie was pleased that he would be taken away from this stand, even if only temporarily. He risked a quick glance across the walkway, under the guise of looking around. A forklift truck carrying a crate hummed past and blasted some diesel fumes at him, making him cough. Beyond the carpet of the stand, the walkways were littered with plastic, pallets and debris. Workmen like himself were bustling to and fro, carrying tools and boxes, each with their own mission. It was warming up inside the hall, and without air conditioning it would be hot later for anyone working on the stands.

Everything around him was drab, noisy and smelly. It was hard to imagine that the show opened in under twenty-four hours and that all this would be clean, tidy and salesy. The girls on the stand opposite stood out as an oasis of bright colours, neat and attractive. As the forklift passed, Jamie could see that another lady had appeared on their stand and seemed to be talking to them as a group. She had the look of a supervisor and was probably giving them their instructions, he thought.

He could now get a good look at them. All were about the same height—quite tall, but that was probably thanks to their ridiculously high heels. He wondered why they were here today, on the set-up day—maybe to practice their sales patter? There were two blonde girls—one with long straight hair, the other shoulder-length—one Black girl with outlandish eye make-up, and the pretty brunette who had pulled her shirt down for him earlier.

Chilly patted him on the shoulder. 'Come on, boy, tea for me, cold shower for you,' he said with a smile, noticing Jamie studying the four girls again.

As he got to his feet, Jamie got a quick whiff of Chilly's body odour, which concerned him. The day was still young and would inevitably get hotter, and their work in the halls had only just begun.

2

After the distraction of the girls on the opposite stand, Jamie didn't feel he had done himself any favours, and as he and Chilly sat down to have a cup of tea, he decided to try to make amends. He had never seen a hall so vast and was fascinated as to what was going to happen here over the next few days. He had heard about exhibitions and expos, but this was his first time at one, and he was genuinely interested.

'How many of these have you been to, Chilly?' he asked.

'Oh ... stacks.'

'How do they work? I don't get it.'

Chilly eyed him, wondering where this question had come from. Most of his apprentice fitters had no interest in the world around them, just beer and girls. He could see in Jamie's eyes that there was a real interest.

'You should ask the boss, Bob; he's been to more of these shows than I've had hot dinners.' He paused, looking around at the noise and bustle that filled the hall. 'These things go on all over the world and all through the year,' he said pensively, 'conventions, exhibitions ... most people just call them expos.'

Jamie nodded and took a mouthful of his tea, but it was too hot. It tended to stay hot in these cardboard cups, and if he was honest, it tasted awful.

'They're a strange commercial institution,' Chilly continued. 'Always held in huge halls just like this. Basically, they're meant to match up products and services with potential customers—and in large numbers.' Chilly turned to face him and smiled. 'It's like the commercial world's equivalent of speed dating.'

Pleased with his analogy, he carried on almost wistfully. 'They offer a single location where one potential customer can browse and compare lots of products, or where one salesman can reach large numbers of potential buyers, with his products right there in front of him and without having to move.' Jamie's mouth had fallen open in a gormless expression, but Chilly took it to mean that he was listening. 'You'll see,' he reassured his young charge. 'They can last from a day to a week or more ... they can be small and "boutique"'—he made air quotes with his thick, sausage fingers—'or absolutely massive—too big to walk around in the time available.'

Jamie pulled out his teabag before the taste became too overpowering. He noticed Chilly had created 'builder's tea' by continually dunking his teabag until the liquid was a rich, deep brown colour.

'Most halls like this,' Chilly continued, 'have a number of entrances, but the past few years they've closed most of them off for security reasons, just leaving the one main entrance.'

'Does stuff get nicked?' Jamie asked.

'All the time,' Chilly confirmed. 'It must be a goldmine for tea leaves here.' Jamie looked confused. 'Tea leaves: thieves,' Chilly interpreted. Jamie was slowly getting used to the rhyming slang Chilly used on a regular basis, but he hadn't heard that one before. 'The robbin' bastards get into a hall like this, with all the stands and booths laid out nicely for them in a lovely grid pattern—it's meant to make best use of the space available, but every stand has valuable junk on it, and it's all loose and easy to take.'

'What about the walkways?' Jamie asked. He seemed to have struck a chord with Chilly, and any sense of urgency to get back to the installations had gone; this was clearly a favourite subject. 'The stands and main walkways look a right mess to me.'

'Well, you've seen the cheap-shit carpet squares they put onto the stands,' Chilly replied, 'the sort of crap you'd find in a school or a library. So if someone spills a coffee or throws up, they just swap out one square.' He smiled. 'Then once all the stands are set up at the end of today, they put down carpet rolls in the main walkways. The aisles are numbered, and sometimes the carpets are colour-coordinated with the aisle numbers to help navigate your way around. But it's still easy to get lost.'

Chilly was obviously very at home in the expo environment. Jamie took a sip of tea. It was truly awful, but it was wet and actually quite welcome.

'You just wait till it gets busy, there are aisles going this way and aisles going that way'—Chilly crossed his arms at right angles to illustrate—'and the junctions are chaotic. People in a hurry bumping into people who're chatting, impromptu meeting points ... You'll see,' he said again.

'Then there's the toilet facilities and catering outlets,' Chilly continued, still idly dunking his teabag. 'They're all round the outside walls, and once the drinking starts at lunchtime, they become meeting points too, particularly in the afternoons after a few beers or a glass of wine.

'So all the sweaty bods here today, like you and me, we're gone tomorrow, replaced by blokes in suits and'—he looked pointedly at Jamie—'girls in skirts.' Jamie pretended not to pick up on the dig, and Chilly continued. 'Today, the day before Day 1, is the set-up day, when the halls are filled with all us fitters, engineers and contractors. We build the stands and make the show ready for tomorrow morning. See those huge roller doors allowing the vans and forklifts in?' He pointed at the far wall of the hall where a pick-up truck was coming in with crates loaded onto the back. 'They'll be closed tomorrow, so no more direct access from outside.' Chilly started to jab the table with his free hand. 'And of course, the tight buggers don't put the aircon on for today—not for us workers, we have to do all the manual labour and sweat it out. They put it on for the rest of the show, though, for all these glossy suited fuckers. Gets bloody hot down here on the floor sometimes, too. Stifling.'

'So what do they sell at these shows? Is it like Comic-Con?'

'Ah, man,' Chilly threw his head back, 'there are conventions and expos for everything.' He paused to think. 'From printing to pastry, superheroes to sex toys, toilets to trombones, you name it, there'll be an expo for it somewhere in the world at some time. Of course, the main reason is to attract the people with projects, money, an obsession or a hobby, and match them up with people who have a product, service or idea that they want to try to sell or promote—or whatever really.'

Chilly finally took a mouthful of his tea. Its strength didn't seem to faze him, and he took a second, longer gulp.

'All sounds a bit shallow,' Jamie commented.

'Oh, it is, completely false, but it's kept me in a job for years, and it's got you away from your Big Macs, so don't knock it. Look behind all the shiny equipment, the free pens and the business suits, and there's a whole industry dedicated to organising, setting up and stripping down these events. Millions of people worldwide are involved in them at some level, just like you and me—and some of 'em are earning a good income from them, too'—he turned to Jamie with a grin—'unlike you and me. Some folk live and breathe them on a daily basis, and yet many people, like my missus for example, will never go to one in their lives. I've been coming to this one for about five years now. They used to call it the Food and Beverage Expo before some bright spark renamed it FaB-Ex.'

'Always here at the NEC?' Jamie asked.

'So far, yes, always here, and always during the summer school holidays. It started in the mid eighties, I think, a year or so before I first came. It varies in size; companies and people come and go; some years are bigger than others; sometimes the weather is hot and sometimes cool and wet; but basically it's always the same.'

Chilly was talking about the expo like it was a family Christmas, but Jamie was fascinated. He couldn't wait to see it all up and running tomorrow.

'Mind you'—Chilly suddenly looked serious—'there's a seedy side to it too.' Once more, he looked pointedly at Jamie. 'Half these blokes in suits are here for a week, away from home, away from their wives and girlfriends, and have no interest in selling anything—to them it's just an excuse to drink and chat up women. Another world with different rules, a false reality they treat as some kind of short-term escape. What happens at FaB-Ex stays at FaB-Ex.'

He looked away again, around the chaos of set-up day. 'Once you've been to an expo like this, particularly as an exhibitor, you see that it can be a strange experience. But it carries on each year regardless, oblivious to what is going on under its roof.'

Chilly was getting melancholy now, and Jamie felt it was time to bring him back to the real world. 'Shouldn't we be getting back to those stands, Chilly?'

Chilly, snapped back from his thoughts, looked at his watch. 'Ooh fuck, yes.'

3

The delays had only got worse. When Jamie and Chilly had reached the other stand that they had to set up, the crates hadn't even arrived. Chilly had shouted profanities and looked quite frustrated before going off to chase the forwarder in the main office. Jamie had been left to wire up some three-phase plugs, which he was happy to do. He had done plenty of these, and he could sit comfortably on the carpet and do them one at a time.

He had been with Haywood Installations now for just over a month and was really beginning to enjoy the work. It was the first 'real' job he had had since leaving technical college the previous September. Bob Haywood, who owned the business, was one of his neighbours and had seen him working in McDonalds. Bob had asked Jamie why he didn't have a 'proper job'—a question that hadn't gone down well with the McDonalds manager who was serving him—and the conversation had led to Jamie being offered the position of apprentice fitter, starting the following week. It was one of those lucky meetings. Jamie had been for over twenty interviews for similar roles, but he was nervous and quiet and hadn't been able to sell himself. Bob had known him for many years, and in fact Jamie used to mow his lawn while Bob and his wife, Judy, were away at their holiday home in Florida.

The pay wasn't great, but it was better than cleaning tables and toilets and it was a job with genuine prospects. In his month so far, he had spent two weeks in the workshop, learning the tools, and since then had been out on-site. He had helped to install a blister packing machine in Widnes and take away some scrap equipment from a warehouse in Eccles. Now he was spending a day and a night in Birmingham at the National Exhibition Centre, setting up these two sales stands and related equipment with his supervisor, Chilly.

He finished the plugs and got to his feet, picking up the wire strands he had left on the carpet, and dropped them in a cardboard box that had become a temporary bin. There was no one else on the stand, just him, some flat-packed brochure racks, a table, some stacked chairs and the blue carpet. He looked at the sign on the front of the stand, which said 'Steelfab Ltd' and the stand number, 'L4'. He guessed he and Chilly would be uncrating some kind of steel equipment and wiring it up to run during the show.

He decided he may as well make himself useful until Chilly got back and set about assembling the brochure stands. As he did so, his mind drifted back to the four girls at the previous stand and how he had been caught out looking at one too closely. The thought made him cringe and smile in equal amounts. Hopefully he wouldn't need to go back there.

Chilly reappeared and seemed a bit more cheery, though his trousers had slipped down again and the crotch wasn't all that far above his knees. Jamie wondered how they actually stayed up.

'Well done, son,' he said, seeing the brochure stands and praising Jamie for his initiative. 'The crates will be here in about thirty, and the compressed air is apparently on at the other stand.' He reached Jamie, finally pulling his trousers up. 'They need to be signed for, so I'll stay here; you go back to the other stand and connect the air up, then check it all works okay. Then come back here and give me a hand setting up.'

'Okay, Chilly, will do,' Jamie said eagerly, starting to leave the stand. It was the first time Chilly had trusted him on his own with live equipment.

Chilly let him get a few metres from the stand before calling after him, 'Aren't you forgetting something?'

Jamie looked back to see him raising his eyebrows and holding out a toolbox.

'Ah, yeah.'

Chilly handed him the metal box and shook his head. 'Heaven bloody help me.'

Jamie really wanted to prove himself to Chilly, and lapses of concentration like this didn't help his cause. He was annoyed with himself.

He was also worried that he would now see those four salesgirls again and made a pact with himself to try to completely ignore them.

4

At dinner that night, Jamie was relieved to see that Chilly had showered and changed into a decent shirt and jeans with a belt that seemed to be working—at least for now. They were staying at the Novotel right next door to the exhibition centre, and there was a half-decent steak house as part of the complex. Chilly had got them each a pint from the bar, which was very welcome, while they looked at the menu.

It had been a long day, but the equipment had all turned up and between the two of them, they had it all up and installed by about 6 pm. At one point in the late morning, Jamie had wondered if they would still be setting up at midnight. However, he was beginning to learn that Chilly's estimates of time to finish these jobs did allow for these delays; it was what the hardened fitter referred to as 'fuck-about time'. Both stands looked superb, all ready to go the next morning. The display equipment was running fine, and Jamie had been over the carpets with a vacuum cleaner he had borrowed, which seemed to please both Chilly and the stand manager.

Chilly had received the sign-off from both companies for their stands and had called Bob Haywood from a payphone to let him know. Jamie had overheard him say to Bob, 'Yeah, the young fella did a great job,' a comment he suspected he wasn't meant to hear but was really pleased with. He ached a bit from moving heavy equipment out of crates and then holding it in position while Chilly fixed it in place, but all in all it had been a good day. He decided he would have the gammon steak and took a big swig of his beer.

On returning to the first stand, he had actually been disappointed to see the four girls had moved on—no sign of them anywhere. Although he had promised himself he would ignore them, he had secretly hoped there would be some more interaction, but it was not to be. He kept an eye out for them as he walked between the halls, but it was just the fitters and stand operators making last-minute adjustments to their layouts or covering things over with sheets in readiness for Day 1 the next morning. As he and Chilly left the bigger hall, the carpets were going down along the walkways, and it was really beginning to look like an expo.

The meals arrived, along with another round of beers. Jamie noticed that Chilly had quite a capacity to put it away. A different person once the jobs were signed off, Chilly was doing most of the talking but still managed to get through his pint faster than Jamie. In the middle of one large gulp, he stopped, froth around his lips.

'Aye aye,' he commented, gesturing towards the door, 'eyes right.' Jamie recognised the laughter and looked round to see the four girls from earlier in the day, heading for the way out. They were dressed more normally now but still seemed to be having a lot of fun. Both men watched them, and Jamie noticed that most of the patrons in the restaurant were men and had been distracted by the activity at the doorway.

The group seemed to be splitting into two, the Black girl and the blonde with long hair telling the other two that they would see them in the morning. Outside the door, the two pairs went off in different directions, and almost as one, the men in the restaurant all turned back to their meals or took a mouthful of their drinks. Jamie did both, then noticed the look he was getting from Chilly.

'What?' he said defensively.

'I guess you're not married yet?' Chilly enquired.

'Ha, no,' Jamie replied as if it were a ludicrous suggestion.

Chilly nodded sagely. 'Just be careful,' he said, 'girls like that in a place like this will chew you up and spit you out.' The pair sat quietly for a while before the older man knocked back the rest of his beer and let out an exaggerated gasp.

'Well,' he said, 'I don't know about you, but I'm knackered, and I'm going to call it a day. Think I'll go back, shed my clothes, crack open a cold one from the minibar and watch some shit on the KY.' The prospect seemed to please him, but he noticed the quizzical look on Jamie's face.

'KY Jelly: telly,' he explained with a smile. Jamie nodded. He really needed to get his head around this rhyming slang.

'Well done today, you did a good job,' Chilly added.

Jamie smiled back at him, pleased with the feedback.

'See you here at 8 am for brekkie, then we'll do a quick once-over at each stand, make it look like we care,' Chilly smiled, 'then we can piss off home.'

Chilly got out of his seat and pushed it back under the table. Jamie, now obsessed with his partner's trousers, sneaked a quick look. They were low and the belt was straining, but they were holding in place—just. He had to stop this and reprimanded himself for his obsession with Chilly's trousers.

'Thanks, Chilly,' he said. 'Really enjoyed it,' he added honestly. 'See you in the morning.'

Chilly gave him a half-wave and patted his stomach appreciatively as he made his way for the exit. Jamie pictured him lying on his bed in his Y-fronts, film on the telly, beer out of the minibar on the bedside table, falling asleep and snoring loudly. The image made him smile.

He too was tired; it had been a long day. He looked at his beer: still half a pint left. He would knock that back and head off himself; he never really felt comfortable sitting at a table on his own. He took as big a sip as he could, but it had been a huge meal and he would need to take his time. He could leave it, but somehow that never seemed right.

A voice from behind him stirred him from his thoughts.

'Hello, you must be Billy-no-mates.'

Jamie looked round to see two of the Wow! girls who'd left a few minutes before, standing at the side of his table—the pretty brunette and the girl with shoulder-length blonde hair. Jamie wasn't sure what to say and just nodded awkwardly.

'Where's your friend?' the brunette asked. Jamie nervously took a sip of his beer.

'The walking arse crack,' the blonde chipped in. This instantly made Jamie laugh, and he spat beer all over the floor and their shoes.

'Oh, I'm so sorry!' he cried, rushing to put his beer back down and grabbing a napkin off the table. He bent down and started to dab at their shoes.

The two girls laughed, both at the comment and also at Jamie's reaction.

'Wow, personal shoe cleaning service,' said the brunette, pulling her foot away. 'You don't have to, it's fine.'

Jamie looked up at her standing over him and caught his breath. He thought she was the most perfect person he had ever seen, and gawped openly at her. 'Please stand up,' she said, 'people are starting to stare.' The two giggled again.

Jamie stood up slowly, his eyes fixed on the brunette girl. 'I thought you'd gone?' He gestured towards the doorway out.

'Yes, we did, but *she* forgot her bag.' The blonde girl wiggled a small clutch bag at Jamie as if in proof, then turned back to her friend. 'Right, shall we try the city, see what the Brum nightlife is like? I'll find a taxi.'

The brunette looked at Jamie. 'No, I won't; you go. I think I'm going to stay.'

'You sure?' The blonde didn't look affronted, more surprised, and looking at Jamie, she added, 'really?'

'Yeah, you go, I'll see you later.' She leaned across and gave her friend a hug and a peck on the cheek, before they parted and the blonde walked out confidently.

'Will she be okay?' Jamie asked, concerned at the thought of a girl on her own in what he assumed from her comment was a strange city.

'You kidding?' the brunette said. 'Look out, Brum!'

Aware they were both standing awkwardly at the side of the table, Jamie asked her if she would like a drink and they drifted across to the bar, which was empty except for a lone businessman at the far end who looked like he was drowning his sorrows. He noticed the two youngsters approach the bar and sneered, knocking back what looked like a neat bourbon.

'Well, Billy,' the brunette answered, continuing the 'no-mates' theme, 'I thought you'd never ask, but since you have, I'd like a white wine spritzer, please.' Jamie nodded, but the barman had overheard and he didn't need to ask.

'Another beer?' the barman asked.

Jamie looked back at his almost-finished and rather sorry-looking pint still sitting on his table. 'Yes, please,' he said.

5

Jamie couldn't work out what was waking him up. Light was streaming in through the open curtains, but it wasn't the sunlight that had woken him up. It was a noise, over and over again ... it must be his alarm clock. He swung his arm out of the bed and across to the bedside table, knocking the lamp and room telephone off onto the floor. The noise stopped. His alarm clock was still there, but it wasn't making any noise. Peace and quiet. His brain struggled to interpret his situation ... and then started to throb. Oh, did it start to throb!

Then he heard a voice, tinny and metallic. 'Jamie, that you? What are you doing, you lazy bugger?'

Chilly ... it was Chilly's voice ... he was calling on the room phone and Jamie had knocked the receiver off, answering it. He scrabbled about on the floor at the side of the bed and ended up falling out in a heap onto the bedside lamp.

'Hi Chilly,' he rasped, his mouth dry and gritty. He cleared his throat and tried to ignore the pounding in his head. 'What's the err, what time is it?'

'I'll tell you what bloody time it is, it's nearly half past fucking eight!' Chilly blasted back, and then continued to give Jamie a verbal roasting. The shouting hurt Jamie's delicate head, and he had to hold the phone away from his ear.

'Oh ... I ... err ...' he stammered, trying to think on the spot, 'I'll go without breakfast this morning. What time shall I meet you?' He felt the nausea rising and knew he had to be quick.

'Nine in the foyer,' Chilly snapped back. 'Don't tell me—you got pissed last—'

He was cut off as Jamie hung up and promptly vomited all over the bed sheets that had been pulled off the bed when he had fallen out. He slumped back against the side of the bed, instantly feeling better, but his head was still humming. He licked his lips, but his mouth was dry and the vomit had left his teeth feeling gritty. He needed some water.

Gingerly, he staggered to his feet and only then saw the full state of his hotel bedroom. Panic-stricken, he looked at the other side of the bed, but there was no one there. The sunlight hurt his eyes, and with his arm across his face he stumbled to the window. He reached it quicker than he had thought and bumped his elbow and penis against the glass at the same time, causing him to jump. He pulled his arm away to see a couple of departing businessmen in the car park two floors below looking up at him. He was naked ... he never slept naked. He cupped his genitals with one hand and whipped the curtain across with the other, feeling some relief from the sunlight and now able to open his eyes fully.

The room was a bombsite. There were clothes everywhere, and the contents of his minibar were on the floor, tables and desk—all empty—along with chocolate, nuts and, rather strangely, the contents of his toolbox.

'Jesus Christ!' he said out loud. 'What happened here?'

He started to remember and winced as the memories came flooding back to him. He and the girl, the brunette, had started out in the bar drinking beer and spritzers before moving on to shots, and then coming up to his room to drink the minibar dry. It had been a wild night—a night of laughter, fun, drinking ... and sex. Lots of sex.

His head was spinning and, realising he was going to vomit again, he rushed into the bathroom and only just made it in time. He spent the next few minutes spitting into the toilet bowl before standing and moving across to the sink for water.

Resting in the sink was a twenty-pound note and, on Novotel paper, a short note in very neat handwriting:

Thank you, Billy

And then underneath, almost as an afterthought:

Same time next year?

FaB-Ex '92

1

The weather wasn't as good this year as the previous year, and each time Jamie went out to the van—which Chilly had been told to park outside the hall, so that the larger vehicles carrying crates could gain access to the main entry doors—he got wet, very wet. It was absolutely tipping down out there, and he cursed each time he needed something he had forgotten on the previous trips. Luckily he had the van keys, so Chilly wouldn't see how disorganised he was.

Jamie had now been with Haywood Installations for just over a year and formally had one more year to run on his apprenticeship before he became fully qualified. His probation period with the company had just ended and he was a full-time employee, but his work still needed to be signed off by Chilly or the customer.

He recognised the hall at the NEC as the same one they had started in last year, but this year, the Steelfab Ltd stand was right at the main entrance to the hall. Jamie imagined it was the perfect place to be, from a sales point of view. The Steelfab stand would be the first that arriving visitors would see as they came through the doors, all fresh and eager to be impressed. Not only had Jamie helped Chilly to set up the Steelfab stand the previous year here at FaB-Ex, but they had also installed four Steelfab units around the country since then. The equipment was simple and Jamie was confident he could do it on his own, so this year he would be solely responsible for the Steelfab stand while Chilly did the other two they were contracted for. Chilly would then have to sign off on Jamie's work at the end of the day, but that was okay.

Once the equipment was all in place and positioned to the satisfaction of the stand staff, Jamie set about connecting it up to power and compressed air. The air would be turned on later in the day, so until then he would assemble the display stands and clean down all the stainless steel, removing his grubby fingerprints from earlier on. The stand staff comprised a middle-aged man, with a suntan and balding head, and his son, who would have been a year or two older than Jamie. The older man owned the company and was teaching his son the ropes; Jamie guessed that this was with a view to him taking over one day. They were nice enough to him, even if they didn't offer him a coffee when they went for one themselves.

At the back of the stand was a small lockable storage area with walls made from the same prefabricated materials as the main stand walls. It was bigger than a cupboard but smaller than a room, and a lockable door at one end allowed valuables to be hidden relatively securely at the end of each day and kept personal items, like briefcases and coats, out of the way during show hours.

'We're going to head off now, Jamie,' said the older man. Jamie was on a stepladder, polishing the steel at the top of their equipment, and made a point of stopping and coming down, out of courtesy. Chilly had told him that building the relationship with the customers was just as important as doing a good job for them. He wiped his hands on a clean rag and nodded. When the man and his son had first arrived at the stand a few hours before, they had both been in suits, but at some point they had changed into blue overalls. The suits had looked good on them; the overalls made them look like something out of a children's TV program or a comedy sketch.

'Yes, of course,' said Jamie. 'I'll be here for a fair while yet, tidying up. I want to make sure it's all nice and clean ready for the morning.'

'Can I leave you to tidy up the floor as well?'

'Yes, of course, it'll be the last thing I do before covering everything up and putting the fencing around the outside,' Jamie replied enthusiastically. The dad had charisma; Jamie could see how he could run his own successful small business but wondered how the son would cope in years to come. The younger man had stayed off to one side with his head down, not wanting to interact with Jamie.

'Good man—and what time do you think you will be here in the morning?'

'I'll aim for twenty minutes before the start,' Jamie answered. He had already worked out his plan for the next day. 'Plenty of time to take the covers off, remove the fencing and get the samples out for you, then I'll head off.'

'Well, you'll be needing this, then,' said the older man, reaching into his overalls and pulling out the key to the lockable door on the storage area. 'Please be sure it's locked before you go today—there's a fair bit of value in there.' Jamie noticed he wasn't wearing a shirt under the overalls and his chest hair seemed wet; he hoped it was from the rain and not sweat, because the key was distinctly damp when he took it.

'I will, of course,' Jamie replied, trying to copy how Chilly would speak to a customer and to be as confident and reassuring as he could. 'Thanks, I'll see you in the morning.' He made a show of closing his hand around the key and popping it into his overalls pocket.

The two men turned and walked away from the stand, the younger man giving Jamie an awkward half-wave as he left. Jamie watched them go out through the main entrance door, blending in with all the other people scurrying around in overalls, and breathed a sigh of relief. He would carry on cleaning and tidying until the compressed air was switched on, but at least now he didn't feel like he was being watched all the time. He checked his pocket for the key, made sure it was safely tucked away, then dropped his cleaning rag onto the carpeted stand, picked up his water bottle and took a big swig. He worked better unsupervised; he was more relaxed and found he made fewer mistakes—probably a confidence thing. He wondered if Chilly would come over to check on him and looked at his watch: 3.45 pm. Now that the two Steelfab guys had gone for the day, sign-off from them would have to wait for the morning.

Jamie sat down at the rear of the stand, his back resting against one wall of the storage area, and took another mouthful of water. He looked up and down the walkways in both directions. A forklift was delivering a large crate to the stand opposite, and there was lots of beeping and an aggressive man directing the driver where to drop it. He remembered the events of twelve months ago and the four girls on the Wow! stand, and wondered if Wow! were here again this year. Once he had finished, he would go and have a look at the map on the wall outside the hall.

He thought about the girl he had spent the night with and felt a yearning inside him. He wasn't sure if he wanted to see her again or not, or what he would say or do if he did. It had been one of those moments in his life that he would always remember and wonder about. He had thought about her so often in the intervening twelve months and wished he could remember more detail from the night. He didn't even know her name or where she was from—all he knew was that she had been a front-of-house model for Wow! Catering. He decided he would finish up as quickly as he could and have a look at the map.

It only took him another twenty minutes to finish the steelwork, tidy away the packaging and empty coffee cups, and finally run a borrowed vacuum cleaner over the carpet. He stood back and admired his work—it looked really good.

Taking the key out of his pocket, he opened the door to the storage area and was surprised just how flimsy it was. Any thief with half a mind could break in, and the lock and door were really little more than a deterrent. Inside the storage area were four or five boxes of brochures and smaller equipment, all of which would be put out on show in the morning. There was a fridge, some boxes of bottled water, a couple of six-packs of beer, coffee-making equipment, and pens. The room was tidy and about half-full. Jamie nudged his toolbox in with his foot and closed and locked the door behind him, testing the door handle before walking away.

2

Jamie felt better after washing his hands and throwing some cold water at his face, and he headed for the main foyer, where the map of all the stands was located on the wall next to the main FaB-Ex entrance. The whole area was chaotic, with groups of people coming and going, carrying boxes and trying to get somewhere in a hurry. He pushed his way up to the map and had to stand almost touching it so as not to block the thoroughfare behind him. It took a few seconds, but he found Wow! Catering; it looked like they had a large stand in one of the other halls. The halls this year seemed to be organised into one hall for food manufacturers, one for equipment and one for catering. Steelfab were in the equipment hall, Hall 3, and Wow! were in the catering hall, Hall 5. He pushed his way out through the crowd behind him and headed across the Piazza towards Hall 5.

He felt a twinge of anxiety as he set off. Why was he doing this? Shouldn't he just forget it? What happened last year happened, and that was that; he should leave it as a memory—a good memory—and not try to recreate it. He told himself this but still found himself heading for Hall 5. He would have a quick look and then go and find Chilly, see if he needed any help on his stand. He might also know when the compressed air was going to be switched on.

Hall 5 was huge, much bigger than Hall 3 where he had come from, but there were fewer people, and Jamie noticed that most stands just had tables and chairs rather than bulky equipment. Up ahead, he recognised the colours of the Wow! logo and felt his palms start to sweat. He was nervous at what he might see, whom he might meet. He would walk past the stand, nonchalantly, as if he was just passing by; maybe cast a casual glance in the right direction ...

The closer he got, the more he tensed up; he was nervous and excited at the same time. He took a deep breath and looked across at the stand. He did his best to be pretending to be walking past for no reason, but he had been opposite this stand at the previous show, so of course he would be interested in it. The stand was bigger than it had been the previous year and had a central section that looked like it could be closed off, like the storage area on the Steelfab stand but ten times the size. Around this was seating, modern-looking white plastic chairs and tables, and plenty of colourful banners and posters. There were about ten people on the stand, most of them standing and a couple of girls sitting. Did he dare look closely? A small group of people passing him walked between him and the stand as he passed it, giving him the perfect cover.

It was mainly men, but there were another two girls standing, and the two girls sitting stood up as he passed them. The long-haired blonde and the Black girl definitely looked like the girls from last year. He looked at the other two, but their faces were hidden. He had gone past the stand now and it would look strange to be staring back over his shoulder, so he looked forward and, without thinking, turned left at the next junction of walkways. His heart was pounding; he felt like he was doing something illicit. He still felt the mixture of nervousness and excitement. Jamie took a deep breath and turned, almost on the spot. He would do one more walk by and this time he would be brave and simply look.

His palms were clammy, and he wiped them on the sides of his overalls legs as he approached the Wow! stand for the second time. The four girls were now all standing in a group on their own. He could see the two girls he had already identified with their backs to him and tried to concentrate on the other two, who were facing him but engrossed in conversation. Three were in jeans and a T-shirt, the fourth was in her Wow! skirt and top. Both the other girls had fair hair; one looked like the short-haired blonde from last year ... Jamie's attention turned to the fourth girl—was it her? She wasn't brunette, more like a strawberry-blonde, but she was the right height and it could quite easily be her. He just couldn't be sure. He was annoyed with himself for being so cowardly.

Enough was enough—he would go and find Chilly; time to move on. Relieved at making the decision, he felt himself relax immediately and turned left after the Wow! stand towards the Hall 5 entrance.

Back on the Wow! stand, the girl with shorter blonde hair nudged the strawberry-blonde on the arm to attract her attention and pointed discreetly at Jamie as he walked past the end of the stand. The strawberry-blonde girl looked at her friend and then in the direction she was pointing, just seeing Jamie in profile as he disappeared around the end of the stand.

3

Back in Hall 3, Jamie had found Chilly on one of the two stands he was responsible for and had helped him with lifting a couple of the heavier items into position. While he was there, one of the organisers had come and advised that the compressed air would be switched on in two minutes. He had waited until it came on and watched Chilly testing the valve, then set off back to the Steelfab stand to do the same there. It was his last job of the day. He had told Chilly that the two Steelfab guys wouldn't be back until the morning, so sign-off would have to wait until then, and arranged to meet Chilly in the Piazza in half an hour.

The halls were pretty empty now as he walked back. Most stands were ready for the next day, though a few still had frantic last-minute tidying going on. He realised as he walked back that he was disappointed with himself and pulled a face as he cursed himself for being so spineless. Never mind, that was who he was, and he had to accept it. It would spare him any more grief from Chilly, who had laced into him the previous year. Although Chilly hadn't known that there was a girl involved, it had been obvious that Jamie had been the worse for alcohol, and Chilly had chastised him for getting so drunk, going on to tease him in the following weeks each time they had had a drink together after a job.

Back at the Steelfab stand, it was exactly as he had left it. He lifted the flap of carpet at the back of the stand to reveal the air valve underneath. He gripped the handle and the body of the valve in his hands and tried to rotate the handle, but it wouldn't budge. He tried a couple of times, but the hard edge of the well-used handle was digging into his skin. He needed his toolbox.

Fishing in his overalls pocket, he pulled out the key, opened the flimsy door to the storage area and went in. The toolbox was on the floor in front of him and he bent over, opened it and rummaged around for the offcut of copper pipe that he used to help open stubborn valves. It wasn't used often and he could see it right at the bottom, under all his other, larger tools. He reached in, grabbed one end and pulled it out, bringing two adjustable spanners and a small hammer with it. He tutted to himself and stood up, then gasped as he felt two hands reach around his face and cover his eyes.

Jamie dropped the pipe in surprise and instinctively tried to turn around, tripping over the toolbox, falling against one of the weak side walls and ending up on the carpeted floor on his back. Standing over him, laughing at him falling, was the girl from the year before. Jamie's face was a mixture of shock and pain—he had landed on the hammer, which he pulled out from under his back with a grimace, then looked up and couldn't help but start to laugh along with her.

'Hi Billy,' she said, 'on your own again?'

Jamie didn't know what to say—he was both excited and terrified to see her again, and this must have registered clearly on his face.

'Oh, I'm sorry, I didn't mean you to hurt yourself.' Then, teasing, 'It's okay, I'll kiss it better.' It *was* her who had been the one of the four that was in the Wow! uniform, with short skirt and low-cut T-shirt emblazoned with the Wow! logo and the tacky tag line 'for all your needs'—the 'catering' seemed to have been dropped altogether this year.

'You've changed your hair?' was all that Jamie could think to say. She was now straddling him. From where he was lying he had a clear view of her knickers, and despite desperately trying not to, he couldn't help a quick look—which she saw. He was ashamed of himself.

'Yes, I have,' she replied and, reaching down, tapped her crotch playfully. 'All of it—look, I'll show you.'

Jamie found himself backing away and ended up putting his hand into his toolbox, which hurt as a pair of plyers pinched his thumb. He whipped his hand out and put his thumb in his mouth to suck the skin. She had stepped away from him and was closing the door, the whole frame shaking as it clicked shut, then turned the snib on the inside to lock themselves in. Jamie looked at his thumb; there was a painful red line that would probably become a blood blister. He looked up at her as she knelt down in front of him.

'I'm sorry,' she said, 'I didn't mean to shock you—or to hurt you.' She tenderly reached out and cupped his face before kissing him on the lips. 'But it's lovely to see you again.'

4

Chilly had got fed up waiting in the Piazza and, picking up his toolbox, had made his way to the Steelfab stand, the metal box clanking as he walked. What was holding up the young man? He was generally quite reliable.

As he walked onto the stand, his toolbox clanked—a very distinctive sound—and he dropped it onto the carpet at the back against the wall, clearing his throat as he looked around. There was no one there, and he sighed.

'Where've ya gone?' he said out loud to himself, then thought he heard a noise from the storage area. If he didn't know any better, it sounded like a girl giggling. He walked to the door of the storage area and tested the handle—it was locked. The amount the whole structure moved as he jiggled the handle surprised him, and he raised his eyebrows before testing it once more. The door was definitely locked but not particularly secure.

Turning to the back wall, he lifted the carpet flap to reveal the compressed air valve, took hold of the handle and tried to turn it. It wouldn't shift. He tried a second time, but still nothing. He changed position so that the body of the valve was wedged between his boots, then, gripping the handle with both hands, yanked it hard. It moved through the ninety degrees, and Chilly heard the whistle and fizz as compressed air filled the pipework downstream. He listened carefully—no further noise either from the valve or the pipework. Gripping the body, he took hold of the handle once more and turned it back to its closed position. That was stiff; he wondered how Jamie had managed to check it—probably used that piece of copper pipe he carries round everywhere. Anyway, all seemed okay, and he was happy with the job Jamie had done setting up the stand.

Chilly stood upright and blinked as a wave of dizziness passed over him. Head rush—he'd stood up too quickly, which had happened a few times recently. As he bent to pick up his toolbox, he consciously did it more slowly to avoid the same thing happening again. The toolbox clanked as he did so, and he shook it to get a better grip.

One last look around the stand. Was it his imagination or did he just see the wall of the storage unit move? He watched it for a few seconds, but nothing more. Must just be the dizziness—it had been a long day. He took a deep breath and set off along the walkway towards the Piazza, toolbox clanking with each step.

5

Chilly was barely at the next junction when the flimsy storage area door opened and the young couple tumbled out together. She was pulling up her knickers and straightening her hair; he was very red in the face and was trying to get his arms back into his overalls. Thankfully, there was no one there to see them spilling out onto the floor.

'Was that your friend?' she asked. 'The arse crack?' They both started laughing, before she took hold of his hand. 'Sorry, I'm sure he's lovely.'

'He is,' Jamie confirmed, 'I've got a lot to thank him for.' He looked at the girl in front of him as she gazed back into his eyes. He thought she was beautiful, really beautiful. He felt his heart start to race. He had so much to ask her.

They both heard the noise at the same time, the clanking toolbox was returning.

'Shit!' Jamie's eyes opened wide. 'He's coming back.' He finally managed to get his arms through the armholes as she straightened her skirt and pulled her shirt down as best she could. The clanking was getting louder, but they couldn't tell exactly how far away he was.

'Hide,' Jamie said. 'I'll come back for you.' She nimbly jumped to her feet and was round the corner of the stand and out of sight just as Chilly appeared at the other corner.

'Where've you been?' he demanded, out of breath.

'Oh, had to nip to the toilet,' Jamie replied, thinking on his feet. 'Just locking my toolbox away.'

'You always take it to the toilet with you, do you?' Chilly asked. 'And why are you all red in the face? Need more fibre in your diet, mate.' Both men thought they heard a quiet giggle and looked towards the corner of the stand, but there was no one there. Jamie stood up and dusted himself down, choosing not to answer either question.

Chilly's demeanour changed. 'You've done a good job here, young fella,' he said. 'I think you've earned a reward ...' He paused as Jamie raised his eyebrows in anticipation; he had heard this line a hundred times before. 'You can buy your boss a pint. Now come along ...'

Jamie turned the key in the storage room door, tested it, and turned back to face Chilly.

Behind Chilly, on the walkway, a pretty girl in a tacky, revealing uniform was walking away from the stand. She glanced over her shoulder and gave Jamie a wave before turning at the next junction and disappearing out of sight.

FaB-Ex '93

1

For the third year running Jamie was setting up the Steelfab stand, and for the second year running he was trusted to do it on his own. He was now fully qualified and certified to sign off the work, but he still lacked confidence and experience.

The hall was the usual scene of chaos, and the stand he was working on was an oasis of calm. The stand was at the junction of walkways, and it annoyed Jamie that occasionally people would use it as a shortcut to turn the corner. It was mid afternoon; he had completed both stands he was responsible for and the compressed air and electric were both fitted and tested. All he had left to do was wipe the equipment down, borrow a vacuum to run over the carpet, then rope off the stand. He decided he deserved a break—a few minutes watching the world go by and a few sips from his bottle of water—and then one last push to get it all finished.

He picked up his bottle and sat with his back against a large process vessel, which was actually comfier than he had expected. He looked across at the long, narrow stand opposite. Each stand was made up of three-metre by three-metre blocks, so he imagined that one was three metres deep by twelve metres long, backed up against an outside wall. There were two men working down the far end of the stand, past the T-junction of the walkways, but otherwise the stand was empty, just a stack of briefcases and coats up at this end.

Jamie took another swig of water and looked at his watch; he'd carry on at 4 pm. He was distracted by the noise of a forklift truck going by and looked back at the stand opposite just in time to see an arm appear and push through the back wall, between the partitions. Jamie watched, unsure quite what he was seeing. The arm groped about in open air before settling on the stack of briefcases, then ran round the edge of the top one until it found the handle, and in the blink of an eye lifted it and pulled it through the gap in the back wall.

Jamie was on his feet in a flash, his water bottle falling to one side onto the carpeting.

'Hey, stop!' he called out, and then to the two men working further along the stand, 'Hey, someone's just nicked your briefcase!' The two men looked up at him but didn't seem to take in what was happening.

'Your briefcase,' Jamie repeated, 'it's gone!' He pointed at the stack of cases while running towards them. The two men dropped everything and ran towards him. 'I saw someone take it,' he explained. 'Their arm came through between the panels at the back, just pulled it through and ... gone.'

All three could see the damaged panel behind the stack of coats and briefcases. The first man peered through the gap.

'There's space behind here, wide enough for someone to get into.' All three men then had the same thought and looked to see where the false back wall ended. At one end was one of the large roller doors for vehicle access, and at the other was one of the many blocks of toilets.

'The big doors, he's gone out of one of the big doors!'

They ran towards the main access door. There were a few people carrying in a large piece of steelwork, and a forklift loading a truck, but otherwise no one.

'The toilets!' Jamie shouted. 'He must have gone the other way to the toilets.' The three ran back into the hall and turned in the opposite direction towards the toilets at the next junction of the walkways.

2

Jamie had found the missing briefcase in one of the toilet cubicles, but everything of any value was already gone. He had returned it to the man from the stand opposite, Jeremy, who had then asked him to go to the security office to help him report it. Jamie was happy to and felt obliged to, but that was the end of his early finish.

Sitting in the security office, he gave his name and contact details and then recounted what he had seen. The security officer, George Worsnip, was a serious man, probably in his fifties, balding and overweight; it crossed Jamie's mind that he would be very easy to outrun. George told them that they believed it was an organised gang, as it appeared that three or four heists had all been pulled off at exactly the same time. They had probably scouted round the hall earlier in the day to pick their targets and then agreed a time to do it, so they could all get away at the same time. Jeremy was told that the best thing he could do was report it to the police and cancel his credit cards as soon as he could; the gang were probably on the M42 by now and would try to use the cards quickly before he could get a chance to cancel them. He and Jamie swapped details, and he thanked Jamie profusely for his help before running off to make the necessary calls.

Jamie stood up. He needed to go, too; Chilly would be wondering where he was. As he opened the security office door he almost walked straight into a girl coming in, and both apologised before recognising each other—it was the girl, the Wow! girl. Behind her were the two blondes, both of whom looked pretty upset.

Jamie stepped back and stood to one side as the three ran in, and two of them started talking agitatedly to the security officer at the same time. Jamie gathered that one or both of them had also had a bag stolen. He wasn't sure whether he should leave or not; he wanted to speak to the girl, but perhaps this wasn't the right time. George looked very flustered, Jamie's presence here wasn't helping, he saw no opportunity to speak to her, and he knew Chilly would be getting anxious.

'Erm ... I'll make a move then,' he said to the security officer, who barely heard him over the shouting.

The girl, whom Jamie noticed had her hair now back in what he assumed was its natural brunette colour, held a finger up as if to say, 'Wait a second'. He then saw her lean over and write something on a nearby yellow sticky note before tearing it off and handing to him, reaching around the backs of the other two girls. No one else had seen the interaction.

Jamie took the yellow sticky note and read it: *344, 9 pm*

He looked up at her, but she was trying to calm her two friends down and was looking the other way. The security officer clearly needed some order if they were to make any progress on this latest theft. Jamie moved quietly out of the room and took one last glance back before pulling the door shut. Just as it closed behind him, he saw her turn quickly and give him a sly wink.

3

Jamie woke before first light. He had made a point this time of not drinking as much as their first night together and had downed a lot of water before finally going to bed in the early hours, and now as a result he needed to go to the toilet. He still felt a bit rough, so he must have drunk a fair bit, despite his promise to himself.

He allowed a minute or so for his eyes to get used to the darkness. The bathroom light was on, casting a strip of light against the far wall and illuminating the room to some extent. He turned his head to one side and could see her asleep in bed facing away from him. If he used her bathroom, he would almost certainly wake her, either by opening the door or by flushing the toilet.

He needed to go, though, and it was becoming more imminent. Turning his head the other way, he could see his clothes draped over the armchair next to the bed. Carefully peeling back the sheets, he swung his legs out of bed as slowly and quietly as he could, then stood up and moved across to the armchair. A bit of rummaging and he found his boxer shorts and shirt and slid both on, his eyes fixed on the girl in the bed, being sure not to make any noise. All that was left were his shoes, socks and trousers. He pulled the socks out of his shoes and slipped them on, then picked up his trousers as quietly as he could. The shoes were lace-ups and he couldn't risk trying to tie them up in the dark, so he would just have to shuffle out.

He felt in his jeans pocket; his watch and wallet were both there, so he made his way towards the door. As he passed the strip of light coming out from the bathroom, he held his watch up to see the time: 4.12 am.

A thought struck him: he should leave a note, like she had done. On the desk by the door, he saw a pen and picked it up; now he needed some paper. He didn't want to open a drawer, as it could be noisy. There was a docket on hotel paper towards the back of the desk, and he pulled it forward into the strip of light so that he could see, then opened the pen and wrote,

Same time next year?
BNM

As he slid the docket back to where it had been, he noticed it was the reservation for the room and pulled it forward again, moving it around in the strip of light until he could make out the name at the top. It said 'N Dawson'.

He still didn't really know her name.

He pushed the docket back into place and quietly opened the room door. The outline under the covers hadn't moved as he walked out into the corridor in shirt and boxers, allowing the door to click behind him as gently as he could, and shuffled off back to his own room.

FaB-Ex '94

1

Bob Haywood had called Jamie the night before to say that Rod Williams, the other senior fitter, couldn't make it to the NEC. Jamie and Rod were rostered to do the set-ups, and this year there were six of them. Jamie was chosen because of his relationship with Steelfab; he knew their equipment like the proverbial back of his hand, and the other companies' equipment wasn't too different. Three set-ups for one person in a day was relatively easy, but six would be close to impossible. With Chilly off work on long-term sick leave, there was simply no one else available for him to call upon.

'Do what you can,' Bob had said, 'and the apprentice and I should be there around 3-ish. We can do all the polishing and tidying up, if you can make a start on them all.'

What could Jamie do? He was stuck with it, so he planned to get in as early as he could and make a start on uncrating for each of the stands. Since he finished his apprenticeship the year before, Bob had been sending him out to jobs on his own to build up his confidence, so he was used to dealing with situations on-site—but this would be a real stretch.

He was staying at the Novotel, as always, and was down to breakfast at 6 am when the kitchen opened. A quick coffee with two slices of toast and he was at the back entrance to Hall 3 just after 6.40 am. To his surprise the doors were open, and there were already people unloading. He managed to get a good spot for the van, close to the door but out of the way of the bigger lorries that would block it later in the morning. In some ways this was better; he was in no doubt as to what he had to do today, and he preferred to work on his own. It probably came from being an only child, but Jamie did enjoy his own company and worked best when he was both on his own and under pressure. In a strange way, he was looking forward to today.

The one thing he might now have to cut out would be his annual pilgrimage to the Wow! stand. Would she be there for a fourth year in a row, and would he see her? He still didn't even know her full name, and yet each time he thought of her he felt excited, even exhilarated. Maybe he could drop by at the end of the day; but his priority was his work, so he would have to see how things went.

There were two stands belonging to companies that Rod Williams usually dealt with and Jamie had no experience of; he would start with them and probably do Steelfab last, as he could set up their equipment with his eyes closed.

He picked up a hall map and, with a marker pen, ringed the six stands he had to set up. All but one of the six were in the smaller equipment hall, Hall 3. This would help, and he did a quick tour of these five. Only two had had their crates delivered, so he set to work immediately on one of these, opening the crate and rolling the equipment out. Then he had to work out how it went together and guess where it was to be positioned. He did his best, but without a photo of the completed set-up and no one there to advise, he couldn't work it out and was aware that he was wasting time. He moved the crate to the edge of the stand and wrote 'PLEASE REMOVE' on a piece of A4 paper, pinned it to the crate and moved on to the next stand.

This was the other one of Rod's, and he was faced with the same situation. Perhaps he should have started with the equipment he knew and done Rod's last? Time was passing way too quickly, and he didn't seem to have made any headway. Jamie could feel panic rising in him.

The third stand was one of his own, and he was able to uncrate it, move the equipment into place, and have it all built and coupled up relatively quickly. One done, and onto the fourth, another of his. He could see the Steelfab stand opposite, with the crates now sitting waiting for him. He was beginning to feel more positive—that was until he looked at his watch: it was already past midday. 'Shit!' he muttered to himself. No time to sit around.

After assembling the equipment at the fourth stand, he went to couple it up to the compressed air line, but the half-coupling necessary to make the connection was missing.

'Shit!' he said again, this time out loud. He wasn't convinced that he had a spare in the van and paused for a minute to think. This was the sort of delay that, had he only had three stands to do, would have been no more than a pain, but today it could end up becoming a major issue for him.

As he stood thinking, the staff for the fourth stand turned up and started putting their bags down. One man approached him, a stern look on his face.

'You from Haywood's?' he enquired. Jamie nodded and offered his hand. 'This all you've done?'

Jamie tried to explain, but the man wouldn't listen. He didn't *care* that Jamie's workload had doubled; as far as he was concerned, his stand was the only one that mattered and was Jamie's top, if not only priority. When Jamie mentioned the missing air coupling, the man simply shrugged and suggested, 'You'd better get it sorted, then, hadn't you?'

As he stepped to one side, Jamie saw two more men approaching and recognised the blue overalls. It was Bradley Copchase, the managing director from Steelfab, and—beside him as always—his son. Jamie still didn't know his name, even after three years of working with them. Chilly called him the Charisma Kid or Mini-Me. Right now neither of them seemed too happy.

'Morning, Mr Copchase,' Jamie offered.

'Morning?' Bradley replied. 'You may not have noticed, young man, but it is now the afternoon.' His tone was accusatory, and he had not taken Jamie's hand to shake it, instead gesturing towards the crates on his stand. 'You haven't even managed to get our equipment out of its crates. Just because Mr Winterbottom isn't here to supervise you is no excuse to be lazing about.'

Jamie could feel the panic rising again and nodded. 'Sorry, Mr Copchase, I'll be straight over to get started.' Chilly always called him 'Cockface', and Jamie had to be careful to pronounce his name correctly to his face. Up until now, Bradley had always been nice to him, but this was a reminder that to him Jamie was still just a contractor. As they turned away, Mini-Me gave him a look as if to say, 'That's told you'. They had to step around someone else coming towards him, and Jamie felt his shoulders slump. Who was this now? Who else wanted a piece of him? The day wasn't going well.

To his amazement, it was the girl—his girl. She had found him. He was aware that he was sweaty and wiped his brow on his sleeve as she stepped up to him.

'Hi, Billy,' she said, a genuinely warm smile on her face. 'Still no mates?'

'None at all today,' he said, 'I've been abandoned.'

'How about a break?' she offered. 'Come and have a coffee.'

She had started to run her hands down the button-up front of his overalls. Jamie noticed her hair was still its natural brunette, and she looked exactly the same as when he had first seen her on the Wow! stand three years ago; she didn't seem to have changed at all. Today, though, she was in a long flowery summer dress, which seemed to bring her sparkly blue eyes to life, and he struggled to take his own eyes off her. He was torn, but he had a job to do.

'I just can't,' he said, 'I'm sorry.'

Behind her he saw Bradley Copchase looking back at him and, noticing that he seemed to be distracted, starting to come back, the 'Charisma Kid' following suit. At the same time, the man in charge of the stand he was on started on him again.

'Now I see why you've got fuck-all done,' he barked. 'Come on, son, you've got a job to do here.'

She took his hand. 'Come find me as soon as you're free for a coffee,' she said, 'I reckon you'll be needing one.'

Jamie cracked, the pressure of being pulled in three directions finally getting to him.

'No!' he snapped, pulling his hand away from her. 'Can't you see I've got things I've got to do? Now leave me alone!'

She looked crestfallen and, bowing her head, turned and walked away without replying.

Jamie immediately felt awful and sighed as she walked off, holding his arms out in a gesture of apology that she didn't see. Jamie watched her walk round the end of the stand and disappear, her head still bowed. He felt terrible, almost physically sick. What had he just done?

'Any time today would be good,' he heard Bradley snarl.

2

By the time Bob Haywood and his young apprentice turned up around 3.30 pm, Jamie had made headway. The fourth stand with the grumpy owner was now completed. Jamie had pinched the air coupling from the Steelfab stand and told Bradley that whoever had packed the crate must have forgotten to include it, knowing that Mini-Me had packed the crate. He had then returned to the first two stands and, running on adrenaline, had managed to work out how to assemble the equipment and connect it up. Essentially, this just left the stand in the other hall, and all the polishing and cleaning up.

Bob had smoothed things over with Bradley and the personnel on each of the other stands, explaining what had happened. He'd then asked Jamie if anything still needed doing that he and the apprentice could help with. Jamie had asked him to try to get a half-coupling for the air on the Steelfab stand from somewhere and, without thinking, had handed him—his boss and the owner of the company—a bundle of rags and the stainless steel polish. Bob willingly took them but passed them straight to his apprentice, who set to work polishing the process equipment without question. Jamie smiled as he looked at the young man; that was him just two short years ago.

For the first time that day he took a deep breath; it was coming together. He looked at his watch: just after 4 pm.

Then he remembered what had happened earlier and cringed inwardly. He was such an idiot. She simply hadn't deserved to be snapped at; she was just trying to be friendly, trying to help. He remembered her smile, the smile he hardly knew and yet knew so well, the smile he saw in his dreams and in his quieter moments throughout the year. He wondered now if he would ever see it again. He would understand if he didn't; he had been a pig to her.

Jamie set off for Hall 5 and the final stand of the day. If it was in the catering hall, then chances were that it was mainly tables and chairs, possibly some stands to assemble, but with any luck nothing major. At one point, as he crossed the Piazza, he felt he was being watched and looked round, but he couldn't see anyone he knew. Was she there somewhere, hurt and offended? He wondered if he would get the chance to apologise to her.

The last stand was big, and there was no one there. This could be either good or bad news, especially at this late stage in the day. No crates, just a huge pile of large cardboard boxes that looked like they had been re-used a number of times, judging by the amount of brown tape on them. Jamie dropped his toolbox and took out the box cutter, then started on the mass of tape that ran along the edges, getting frustrated when it stuck to his fingers and he couldn't drop it onto the floor. As he had thought, mostly tables, chairs and display stands—these would be easy, just time-consuming.

He was able to empty the boxes on his own, flatten them and put them all in the rear storage area. It reminded him of his amorous adventures on the Steelfab stand the year before last, and he felt a twinge of excitement—until he remembered once again what he had done a few hours before, and his mood swung back. In one of the boxes, he found a proposed map of the stand, showing the positions of all the tables, chairs and stands. *Great!* It meant he didn't need to think, and within an hour he had the stand looking superb.

He borrowed a battered-looking vacuum cleaner from a stand close by and gave the carpet a once-over before emptying the bag and returning the vacuum cleaner to its owner, who commented that it was probably the first time it had ever been emptied. Finally, he covered the tables and stands with some blue sheets he found in one of the boxes, then moved some of the chairs to the perimeter of the stand and ran tape around them as a deterrent to it being used as a short cut. Jamie stood back and, in an exaggerated movement, dusted his hands, admiring his work. It did look good.

'Really well done, Jamie,' said someone behind him, and he turned to see Bob and the apprentice approaching. Bob patted Jamie on the shoulder. 'I am so sorry you had all this to do yourself, but thank you so much—you really have done a great job, young man.'

Bob went on to say that the missing air coupling was now on the Steelfab stand and that he couldn't fit it himself as he had no tools, asking Jamie if he could please pop back and fit and test it. Jamie agreed; he was relieved that such a simple job could round off his day, after the nightmare he had been through earlier on.

'Now,' Bob continued, 'with no Rod here, can I ask you to go to Tamworth first thing tomorrow to do his installation job there, please?'

'What about the sign-off here?' Jamie asked.

'I'm going to stay tonight,' Bob explained, 'so I can do that, but I can't do the Tamworth job.' Jamie nodded as Bob gave him a slip of paper with the details on and again put his hand on the fitter's shoulder. 'Thank you again, Jamie. Any other job we could simply have postponed, but with FaB-Ex we can't—and I'll see that you are well paid for all of this.'

Jamie nodded. He knew Bob would be good to his word.

The men parted company, Bob commenting that he owed Jamie a beer and would see him later in the bar, and Jamie headed back to Hall 3 to fit the Steelfab airline. The pressure now off, he felt exhausted. His arms were aching and he had a headache starting, probably from not eating or drinking any water during the day—he had just pushed on. He kept replaying the incident with the girl in his head, and each time he reprimanded himself for losing it with her. He was so angry with himself for his lapse and felt like there was a dark cloud hanging over him.

It was well after 6 pm now and Hall 3 was empty, except for a few forklifts taking crates away. The walkways were being swept and cleaned and the carpets laid along them. This was when Jamie liked these halls: when they were set up and ready but had no people in them. He felt this was his world; he felt quite at home here.

Arriving at the Steelfab stand, he found the coupling and fitted it, connected it up and tested it in under two minutes, then flopped back against the back wall—which moved disturbingly under his weight—and closed his eyes. What a day.

'So, did it get any better?' Jamie opened his eyes to see the girl standing in front of him. The light from the main entry door was directly behind her, giving her a halo and the appearance of an angel. He blinked and put his hand across his face.

'You came back?' he said in disbelief.

'Yes,' she replied, 'I came back,'—then, after a slight pause and with a cheeky grin—'like a bad penny, as my dear old grandma would have said.'

Jamie was so delighted to see her, he didn't know what to say at first. 'I am so sorry,' he said, 'you didn't deserve that. I shouldn't have shouted at you. I'm such an arsehole.'

She knelt down next to him and kissed his forehead. 'You're not an arsehole,' she said, 'I just picked a bad time. I should be apologising to you.' She sat back against the wall alongside him. The wall moved a bit more than she had expected, and they exchanged a look of surprise. Jamie rested his head on her shoulder, which at that moment seemed the most natural thing in the world to do.

'Where's your friend today?' she asked. 'The guy you usually come with.'

Jamie closed his eyes and kept his head resting on her shoulder. 'Chilly?' he said. 'He's off work for a few weeks. The doctor says he's got acute angina.'

'Oh, I've got one of those,' she quipped, making Jamie laugh, before continuing, 'I'm sorry to hear that. He seemed a nice man, protective of you.' Jamie thought this was very astute of her, considering how little she would have seen of Chilly. 'My granddad has the same thing; he just takes tablets,' she said, 'but every now and then he's bedridden for a few days.'

There was a long pause, and then she asked, 'Why do you call him Chilly?'

'It's short for Chilly-Arse,' Jamie answered without opening his eyes.

'Oh, really? Is that because it's always out in the open?' Her innocent question made Jamie laugh again, but he still kept his eyes closed. He loved her honesty.

'I hadn't thought of that,' he replied truthfully. 'No, it's because his surname is Winterbottom.'

She giggled at her own question, now able to see the sense of the nickname.

Jamie was so pleased to see her. Despite what had happened between them, there was an innocence about her that simply made him relaxed and comfortable. The relief that she hadn't taken his earlier sharpness to heart was simply palpable. He just wanted her to keep talking, so he could listen to her voice. She smelled so good, too—he dreaded to think what he smelled like. It didn't take long before he fell asleep; he was so exhausted. His head was now really heavy, and she adjusted her position so she was lying flat on the carpet. He lay on his side with his head resting on her chest, while she stroked his hair.

3

Jamie's alarm went off at 6 am, and he reached across to turn it off. It took him a few seconds to gather his thoughts while he remembered where he was and what he was doing there. He spun over in bed, his arm feeling to his left—but there was no one there. The sheets had been pulled back neatly. He sighed; she had gone again.

He rubbed his eyes and thought about the day ahead. He had to be in Tamworth for 9 am to do Rod's installation. He cursed his bad luck. Under normal circumstances he would have stayed at the NEC and gone round each of the six stands, getting their approval. No matter how grumpy they all were yesterday, stand owners were always upbeat on the first morning of the expo, and he would have dealt with very different people. He could then have gone on and found the Wow! stand.

Unlike the previous years that they had hooked up, when the night-times had been lustful and frenetic, or the knee-trembler two years ago in the Steelfab storage area, last night had been slow and gentle. Their lovemaking had been tender and caring, somehow unlike any other experience he'd had. But now she was gone, like a dream—gone again. She had appeared in his life four times now and changed him a little each time—and yet he knew virtually nothing about her.

Jamie brushed the sheets to his left, the act giving him some comfort, as if her spirit were still there. His hand hit something harder, and he sat up, his eyes straining in the half-light to see what was there. It was a note, written on Novotel paper. He grabbed it and flicked the room lights on, wincing for a second at the sudden brightness. It read,

Thank you, Billy
Same time next year?
Your Bad Penny

FaB-Ex '95

1

Haywood's had four members of staff at the expo this year, and Jamie was relieved that he wouldn't face the same issues as the previous year. The apprentice who had not long started with them at FaB-Ex last year had gone, as had Rod Williams, the unreliable fitter who had let them down. Bob Haywood had let them both go; the apprentice simply didn't make the grade, and he couldn't have fitters who didn't turn up. In their place he had taken on another apprentice, a young lad called Craig who seemed eager to please but for now lacked technical know-how. He was studying two days a week at the local technical college, so hopefully that would change.

Chilly was back in the team but on reduced duties. Jamie was so pleased to have him back; his technical experience and natural ability with people gave everyone around him confidence. His angina was under control, but he could only supervise—no heavy lifting or stress—and it was Jamie's responsibility to make sure he stuck to this. It was hard, because if Chilly saw anything being done incorrectly, his first reaction was to jump in and help.

Finally, there was Bob Haywood himself. He had decided to come along to FaB-Ex to manage the stand operators and personnel so that his staff could get on with the task of assembling, testing and setting up. His experience at the show the previous year had shown him that one person couldn't do it all. Bob was also seriously thinking about actually exhibiting at the expo the next year. After all, where better to display your stand set-up services than at a show where your company has set up a number of the stands?

The workload was growing, and this year they had nine stands to assemble and set up. Jamie would do three, these being the most complex and including Steelfab, as always. Craig would do the next three under Chilly's supervision, and the remaining three, which were in the catering hall, would be easy jobs for Bob or any of the other men to step in and help with once they had finished in the equipment hall.

Jamie had had a busy year. His workload with Haywood's had increased no end, and he had negotiated a new contract with Bob, where he earned a good overtime rate for working weekends, which he did regularly. As a result, he had bought himself a decent car and put a deposit down on a flat about ten minutes away from his parents. He had also started seeing a local girl about two months after the last FaB-Ex, in late September. Alison was the receptionist at one of the local companies Jamie did work for. It had begun when Jamie visited her site a number of times in the one week, and they had chatted while waiting for his host to come down to reception. They had hit it off straight away and agreed to meet up for a drink one evening while Jamie was working there. She was a pretty girl, friendly and outgoing, and Jamie had enjoyed her company and the spark he had felt between them. Bob was good about it and always rostered Jamie to do the work there, even if other fitters were better suited or more available.

The biggest change in Jamie's life, though, which had come as a major shock to him, was that Alison had told him a few weeks ago that she was pregnant. So soon! He had panicked initially, wondering how he was going to look after a young family, but the more he thought about it, the more excited he became at the thought of being a dad. It would be a huge change in his life, and he was trying to convince himself that he was ready for it.

Time on his own at sites or expos like this didn't help. His mind would wander, and he would think about all the possible problems and issues. Alison would have to stop work and move in with him, and all three would need to live in his small flat, at least initially. Overheads would go up and income would come down. Every time he thought about it, he felt a darkness start to shroud him, so he tried to push the thoughts away as soon as they came.

His parents had both taken it well, much better than he had thought they would—at least, they had to his face. It was hard to tell if they were genuinely pleased, but they were certainly making all the right noises, offering to help out with babysitting at weekends or act as a taxi service and so on. He got a knot in his stomach when he thought about being a father and wondered if that was normal. Did all dads-to-be go through this mixture of emotions and feelings?

In the month after FaB-Ex the previous year, he had thought about little else but Penny, dear sweet Bad Penny. But since he had started seeing Alison, he had thought of her less, and since the revelation that he was going to be a dad, Penny barely featured at all.

Being back in Hall 3 naturally reminded him of her, though, and he was interested to know if she was here again this year. He finished his first two stands very quickly indeed, mostly helped by the fact that it was he who had disassembled the equipment at the company sites and packed it into the crates. Just Steelfab to go. He decided he would take a break, buy himself a bottle of water in the Piazza, and wander back through Hall 5, the huge catering hall where the Wow! stand was always located.

The hall map was in its usual place, and he scanned down the list of company names as forklifts ran to and fro behind him. He didn't really notice them any more, and the smell of their diesel fumes as they chugged by was familiar to him now rather than unpleasant.

He couldn't see Wow! on the list and scanned again. At the end of the Ws, it went from 'Workplace Health and Safety' to 'Xellent Ltd'. Wow! wasn't there. He must have checked five or six times before finally moving away and heading off to Hall 3 and the Steelfab stand.

He felt sad, and the emotion surprised him. It showed the impact that one girl had had on him in just four brief encounters. To him, she represented fun and freedom, and he had enjoyed her warmth, energy, honesty and charisma. He had felt truly relaxed in her company.

The Steelfab stand was close to the main entrance again, and Jamie reached it quickly. There was no sign of Bradley or the Charisma Kid on the stand, but Steelfab had taken on a new sales engineer called Don, and Jamie could see him there starting to uncrate the equipment.

Jamie sighed deeply. He couldn't shake the feeling of disappointment. He guessed that was it, the end of that chapter in his life. Perhaps it was for the best; he had Alison now and a new, more challenging life looming. After all, what would he do if he met her again this year? Nothing more could happen between them.

Don saw him approaching the stand and walked across to greet him, shaking Jamie's hand warmly. It was the distraction Jamie needed.

'Right then,' he said, 'let's get cracking.'

FaB-Ex '96

1

She straightened her skirt in the mirror and checked her lipstick: all perfect. She was dressed differently today, a smart grey knee-length skirt and white blouse, the recognised corporate identity. It seemed odd to be here at the NEC and not be wearing that awful Wow! uniform, but hopefully those days were behind her.

The NEC reminded her of Billy—how could it not? She only seemed to come here once a year, for this particular show, and even just walking into the building, the sights, sounds and smells reminded her of him. He was Billy and she was Penny—she smiled at the thought and the memories it brought back. She would have a quick look for him on the way to the stand; he always set up the Steelfab stand, that would be a good place for her to start.

She looked at her watch: 9.15 am. She needed to be at the stand for 10 am and would make a point of getting there early, to show willingness and to help to put the brochures out. She had only been in the job two weeks; there had been a restructure and some of the more competent girls had been re-hired as junior sales staff. So far she had really enjoyed it—it was nice to be recognised for her brain and abilities, rather than her body.

She strode out of the rest rooms and into the Piazza full of confidence and headed for Hall 3. Steelfab was easy to find, right in front of the main entry door to the hall. She had to show her exhibitor's pass as she went through and then draped the lanyard around her neck.

There were three people on the stand: an older man, a nervous-looking younger man, and a sharp-featured, confident-looking man who smiled as she approached. Two of the men introduced themselves to her as Bradley and Don, but the younger man held back. The oldest man commented that she was their first visitor to the stand and that it would be a good expo if this continued. She smiled politely but found him a bit smarmy, and she was relieved when he walked away to speak to another man who had approached the stand.

'Do you mind if I ask who you use to set up your stand?' she asked. 'Or do you do it yourselves?'

'Not at all,' Don replied. 'Bradley tells me he has used the same company for a number of years. I haven't been with Steelfab all that long.'

'Who set it up here for this show?' she asked.

'Oh, err ...' Don turned away, thinking. 'Yes, of course, his name is Craig—youngish guy, just passed his apprenticeship with them, did a great job.' He gestured around the stand at all the gleaming equipment purring away and the furniture neatly set out. As he did so another girl, dressed in the same corporate uniform, walked up to them. The two girls greeted each other, clearly delighted to have met up, and carefully hugged without disturbing make-up or hair.

The new girl turned her attention to Don. 'The show hasn't even started and she's chatting up the best-looking man in the hall.' It was an obvious flirt, and Don seemed pleased with the attention, looking back and forth between the two ladies in front of him. The conversation went on for a few minutes, and they agreed to all meet up again for coffee another morning.

She nodded along with it but her mind was elsewhere, and as the girls parted to head to their own stand, she called back, 'Don, do you know where I can find Craig?'

It took Don half a second to jump back to the previous conversation. 'Oh, he'll have long gone,' he said dismissively. 'He finished yesterday afternoon, all signed off and finished by about 4 pm. He could still be around, but I doubt it. He'll be back the day after the show's finished for the take-down.'

He smiled at her and she thanked him, her head dropping for the first time; she looked genuinely disappointed. He watched as the two girls walked away, thinking to himself that it was a strange reaction, and he would make a note to let Craig know that a salesgirl had been asking for him.

FaB-Ex '97

1

Jamie was pleased to be back at the NEC. It had seemed strange not to be there last year, but it had fallen right at the beginning of his honeymoon, so he hadn't really missed it. Since then, he had worked most weekends, trying to earn as much overtime as he could while Alison was still off work. Although the extra hours brought in good money, it was putting a strain on them as a couple and particularly on Alison, as it meant she became the primary carer for their little boy, Josh. When Jamie was at home, he was exhausted and spent his time either sleeping or doing paperwork. He wasn't happy about not spending weekends with his family, but he really had no choice.

He was hoping Alison would return to work once Josh started at school, albeit a few years away yet. He would only be there a few hours each day initially, so she would have to go part-time, but that would be a start. Perhaps once she got back into a routine, he could look to ease up a bit on the overtime.

He actually hadn't been rostered to work the week at FaB-Ex, but he had Craig to thank for being here now. As soon as Craig had passed his apprenticeship and received his diploma from the technical college he had quietly started to look for another job, and it hadn't been long before he had found a better-paid one. It had been a slap in the face for Bob and Chilly, who had both invested a lot of time, energy and patience into his training. Bob had called Jamie into his office and pleaded with him to let him know with good warning if he was planning to leave. Jamie had reassured him that he wasn't—the truth was that it had never crossed his mind. Bob had got up from behind his desk and, shaking Jamie's hand, had given him a hug, which had really surprised Jamie.

Craig had finished up the week before, which left Bob short-staffed for the FaB-Ex set-up. It would just be him, Jamie and Chilly this year, but they only had seven stands to do, which was a slight drop from previous years. Three of them were in the catering hall, which Bob would do, while Jamie and Chilly set up the other four in the equipment hall.

Being back in Hall 3 with Chilly was like old times. The Piazza had been given a bit of a facelift and seemed a lot brighter, with new eating and drinking outlets dotted around in the manner of a true European piazza. Chilly was still on reduced duties, but Jamie knew the equipment inside-out now and only really needed Chilly to fetch water and coffees or hand him tools while he was underneath some large piece of process equipment. Chilly would talk to the stand owners and personnel while Jamie worked his magic with the set-up and positioning. Bob called them his 'dream team'.

As Jamie returned from the toilets on one occasion, he passed the big hall plan on the wall just outside the main entrance to Hall 3. There were a lot of people gathered around it, all looking for stand numbers, and Jamie, who wasn't particularly tall, had to muscle his way past a few to get close enough to read the text. Without thinking, he found Steelfab listed, then each of the other stands he was working on that day. His eyes moved to the right and lower down, to the end of the Ws—but it was the same as the last year that he had looked; the alphabetic listing went from 'Workplace Health & Safety' to 'Xellent Ltd.' No sign of Wow! He hadn't really expected anything different and started to move back through the crowd towards the main door and the Steelfab stand. As he did so, he brushed shoulders with a couple of women, identically dressed in a corporate style, trying to muscle their way to the front. Jamie muttered a half-hearted apology and kept moving, but the two women, intent on the hall map, didn't even notice him.

As he walked through the wide door into the hall with all its bustle and activity, he had a flashback. A smell, a perfume smell, a scent he recognised ... he was immediately transported back to another time—back to the storage area, back to his hotel room, back to Penny. It was *her* perfume.

Jamie flicked his head round and started scouring the group of people he had just pushed through. It was a large crowd and was constantly moving and changing, with small groups and individuals each on their own mission and heading in different directions. He wasn't sure exactly what he was looking for—brunette hair, strawberry-blonde hair? She could have changed it again. Jamie felt a brief twinge of excitement. Could it be possible that she was here somewhere, right in front of him? As the seconds passed and the people moved out of the group he felt desperate, scanning further out of the crowd in each direction as he moved back towards the map—but nothing. He sniffed the air again—also nothing.

His shoulders slumped with his disappointment. It could have been anyone, not necessarily Penny; she can't be the only person in the world who wore that particular perfume, and by the looks of it there was someone else at FaB-Ex that wore it. He tutted to himself at his reaction and for his brief moment of madness. He had moved on now, that was another life. Time to draw a line under all of this, time to consign his Bad Penny to history.

Back on the stand, Bob had arrived and was chatting to Chilly against the back wall.

'Thank you, dream team,' Bob said to both the overalled men as Jamie approached. 'As always, you've done a fantastic job for me.' Both men nodded in appreciation, a smile of understanding flashing between them.

'And I've made another decision, too,' Bob continued. 'We *will* plan to have our own stand at the show—just a small one, but where better to attract people who need installers than at an expo where all the stands need installing?'

'But the people looking around the show don't necessarily need installers,' Jamie pointed out.

'That's true,' Bob replied, 'but all the decision-makers on these stands go for a walk around at some point, and that's when we pounce.' Bob made an exaggerated gesture like a cat catching a mouse, then smiled at the two men in front of him, both of whom were raising their eyebrows. 'Probably not next year, because all the best spots have been taken,' he continued, 'but maybe the year after.' Jamie and Chilly nodded, both muttering words of approval. 'And I want you two to help me man the stand.'

'All right, Bob,' Chilly took Bob's arm, 'time to get you a stiff drink, old fella.' They all laughed.

'I have a question,' Jamie blurted. The other two men unlinked arms and turned to look at him, expecting a question on Haywood's having a stand. 'Do you remember that stand you used to see here a few years ago—Wow! Catering? What happened to them?'

'Oh, you mean the titty stand,' Chilly laughed. Jamie couldn't explain it, but he almost felt affronted at this comment. It was a typical Chilly remark, but he didn't like it.

'Yes, that's the one,' he reluctantly agreed. 'They were opposite us that first year.'

'The old guy that owned the business sold it,' Bob answered. There wasn't much about these businesses that he didn't know or keep up to date with. 'The man was a dinosaur,' he continued; 'sold his goods on the basis of scantily clad women fronting his stand. It was the same at his offices apparently. He was personally done for sexual harassment about three times, dirty old bastard. Anyway, he reached sixty and decided to retire; made an absolute fortune, I'm told. Lives on an island in the Med now, the lucky bugger.'

Chilly smiled at Jamie. Obviously Bob would have liked to have done the same, but it was unlikely that his business would sell for enough to allow him to buy an island. 'If I remember correctly, it was a management buy-out. Got a bit messy when it went through the courts, so the company sank without trace for a while, but I think they're up and running again now and have re-hired a lot of the old employees. Changed the name, of course, to something more commercially acceptable, less sexist and chauvinistic.'

'I guess their employees don't walk round in short skirts any more with their tits hanging out then?' Chilly flippantly questioned, a cheeky grin on his face.

Once more, Jamie felt affronted but tried not to show it. 'What's the company called now?' he asked.

Bob pursed his lips and looked skyward. 'Sorry, mate, I honestly can't remember.'

FaB-Ex '98

1

Bob Haywood had a lot on his plate, and this year he was at the NEC for the duration of the FaB-Ex show. As he suspected, he hadn't managed to get a good location at the front of the equipment hall this year, so hadn't booked a stand; he had arranged that for the following year. Bookings for work were down though—just six this year—so he needed to walk round the show and try to sell his services. Cold-calling: he hated it. A lot of equipment manufacturers were now hiring internally for their installations, which was hurting his business. Another option, which he had resisted for a long time, was to expand overseas. This brought other problems and was something he would think about if he couldn't drum up business at home.

He had taken on two new fitters at the same time; one was paired up with Jamie and the other with Chilly, but until they could be sent out on their own, they were a burden on him financially. The first, Alan, was fresh out of college, and Bob still wasn't sure about him. The other, Ward, was from New Zealand and had plenty of common sense and motivation. He was a real find.

Chilly had been through another incident with his angina just after Christmas and had been on three days a week since coming back to work in late January. He was a good mentor to the young fitters and new staff, but Bob wasn't sure exactly what he would do with Chilly when there was no one to train. His reduced availability and inability to lift or work in stressful conditions was very limiting. He owed Chilly a lot and felt a responsibility to keep him employed as long as he could. He might try to talk to him about early retirement if the opportunity presented itself.

Then there was Jamie.

Jamie was now his best and most experienced active installer, and from a professional—and, admittedly, selfish—point of view, Bob couldn't afford to lose him. But personally, he was really concerned about Jamie. Normally calm but upbeat and pro-active, Jamie had been uncommunicative and distant in recent months. He wouldn't talk about it, but Bob knew that his marriage was in trouble. He hoped it wasn't the job that was the cause, but the nature of his work meant that Jamie was away from home a lot, especially at weekends. He adored his little boy, Josh, but barely saw him, and Alison was playing the situation by making it increasingly hard for him to see and spend time with Josh when he was around. There was very little that Bob could do, no alternative work he could offer Jamie; he needed him to do the time-consuming and remote jobs. Jamie's only solution would be to leave the job and find something local, but he was a loyal employee and Bob knew he wouldn't leave.

That may have been how Jamie was thinking, but Bob suspected that the marriage would be in trouble irrespective of Jamie's work conditions. Maybe the absence from home was simply accelerating the inevitable? Bob was no expert; he and his wife had married young but had been happy together for thirty-five years.

To compound matters, Jamie's father had just died, about a week ago. His mother had called the office while Jamie was away on a job, and Bob had the unenviable task of breaking the heavy news. Heart attack, apparently. The funeral had been two days before FaB-Ex and Bob had told him to take the week off, ostensibly to be with his mother, but he also suspected that Jamie would be very fragile. He had always looked up to his father, and here was one more pillar in his life that had crumbled away.

Bob would just have to be there if Jamie needed him. As his boss there wasn't much more he could do, but as his friend he was extremely worried. He would make some time on his own this week during the evenings; he would leave Chilly and the two younger men in the bar and excuse himself 'to do paperwork,' because he really needed to give these matters some serious thought.

He draped the lanyard around his neck. It stated that he was 'Blob Hasgood, Manager, Steelfib' and then in small letters underneath, 'Exhibitor'. He knew he had written his name down correctly—how did these people get it so wrong? He was hoping that the fact it said he was an exhibitor would make stand personnel less suspicious of his approaches, and that being listed as a Steelfab employee rather than an installer might also help. Bradley from Steelfab had said he could use their company name as a disguise for his forthcoming sales activities. Bob checked his pocket; a bulky block confirmed that he had plenty of business cards to give out, and the leather folder tucked under his arm contained a large number of the new flyers he had printed out specially for the day's work he had ahead of him.

He cleared his throat, straightened himself up, walked through the main entry doors into Hall 3, and headed for the first large stand with equipment on it. He was a salesman now, and he was on a mission.

2

Five hours later, Bob was exhausted. He would never criticise salesmen again for having a cushy job—this was hard work. He had spent the morning in Hall 3 and then in halls 4 and 5 during the afternoon, and his intention was to do the same again each day for the duration of the show. There was no equipment in Hall 5, but some of the stands these days were like small prefabricated buildings and the personnel who manned them had no interest in putting them together or taking them down. This was a clear opportunity for Bob and his company, and he had made a note to approach some of the companies who actually designed these stands—perhaps he could get in with them.

He had checked in on Chilly and the boys a few times, and all seemed to be going well there, but they were all missing Jamie. He looked at his watch: 3.15 pm. He would call it a day at 4 pm and go for a quiet cup of tea somewhere.

He looked up at the next stand, which was huge. Pastel colours, very spacious, with a luxurious look and very enticing for a prospective buyer. Emblazoned in huge neat lettering over it all, the company name 'Blue Riband Catering' couldn't be missed. The world of expos was changing; big money was being invested in these show stands now, and it was time he got a piece of it.

As he stepped onto the stand, a smartly dressed young lady looked up from a table nearby and asked, 'Good afternoon, can we help you?' Bob's face must have said it all, because with a broad welcoming smile, she continued, 'How about a tea or coffee and five minutes to sit down?' It was exactly what Bob had been dreaming of for the last half hour.

'Yes, please,' he said enthusiastically, 'all of the above,' and plopped down in a chair at the adjacent table.

She stood up. 'No problem. The tea in the urn is a bit stewed, so I'll make you a fresh one and see if I can find any of the good bickies too. If you don't mind, I might join you.' Bob smiled thankfully as he gathered his breath and dropped the bags he had collected onto the floor.

As she walked past to the kitchen area, Bob took note of her appearance. She was medium height, but looked taller because of the heels she was wearing, and dressed professionally. She had shoulder-length brown hair and with her friendly, welcoming manner, Bob felt immediately at his ease. After she had passed him, he got a slight whiff of perfume and breathed it in before chastising himself for behaving like a man half his age. At the adjacent table, where she had been sitting, there was a small clear plastic box full of business cards. He stood up, moved across while her back was still turned, and took one, returning to his original table and sitting down just as she came across with the biscuits.

'Chocolate digestives,' she said. 'We save those for the late afternoon cups of tea. Back in a mo' with the tea. Do you have milk and sugar?'

'Yes, please and two, please,' he replied. Her back turned again, he glanced at the business card and popped it in his top pocket along with all the other cards he had collected on his walks around the stands.

'So what do you do, and why have you landed on our stand?' she asked as she walked back slowly with the two teas and sat down opposite him at the same table, pushing the milky one towards Bob. Her manner was disarming, and Bob found himself opening up to her while she sat and listened, nodding occasionally but always making eye contact. He told her how they were an industrial installers, but business was flagging a bit because he had always relied on word of mouth for his business growth, and perhaps the time had come for him to be a little more pro-active.

He showed her his printed flyers and saw her frown slightly for the first time. 'What is it?' he asked.

'Do you mind if I speak frankly?' she asked. He indicated that he didn't, at which she reached across to the table she had been sitting at and picked up a single-page flyer from a small stack. She lined the two flyers up side by side and moved round the table so that she was next to Bob.

She simultaneously turned the two flyers over; Bob's was blank on the back, whereas the other had beautiful photos of catering scenes, each with one of their cups or disposable items in pride of place.

'Firstly, always use all the space you have,' she said. 'The reverse side is perfect for example photos, and if you are already committed to printing the front, it doesn't cost much more to print on the back.' Bob nodded.

'Secondly—and please don't be offended, but your photos look like holiday snaps. You need bright sharp images that clearly show what you have to offer.' Bob resignedly nodded again before she continued with a few more points. Bob agreed with them all. He had put the flyer together himself in what he thought was a professional and attractive manner, but placed alongside the Blue Riband flyer on the table in front of him, he could now see that it looked more like something a child might have put together.

'Who designed yours?' he asked. 'Were they done professionally? I bet they cost a fortune.'

'I did them,' she smiled. 'I've got a graphic design background, which is why they get me to do their marketing. I absolutely love it.'

Bob nodded, but he felt bewildered. Graphic design? Marketing? When did great customer service at a great price stop being enough?

It must have showed in his face, because she put her hand on his for a brief second in reassurance and looked to her left and right to make sure no one was in earshot.

'I would be happy to redesign these for you—it'll take me about an hour using the blurb from this one'—she pointed to Bob's flyer—'then all you'll need to do is get some good new photos to insert, and I can let you have the file for printing. You won't have them for this show, but the whole process only takes about ten days.'

'What would you charge?' Bob asked, keeping his voice low.

'Oh, I wouldn't charge,' she assured him. 'I'll do it in my room this evening. In fact, we get so much printing done that what we quite often do is piggy-back our clients' printing off the back of our own so they get a good rate too. Consider it all part of the service.'

He frowned as he thought it over.

'No pressure or obligation,' she said, 'but I'd be happy to do it. Have a word with the photographer who wanders round the show—get him to take some shots of the stands you've erected and let you have the digital files.'

Bob had seen the photographer, whom he'd always tried to avoid. Why would he want to be in any of the expo pics?

'He'll charge you,' she continued, 'but you need them. Good pictures sell; bad pictures show a lack of commitment and professionalism and can actually do the opposite.'

Bob raised his eyebrows and nodded at her. She was good—no wonder she was in sales.

'You have a deal,' he said, giving her one of his business cards and offering his hand across the table. She giggled and took both, smiling warmly back at him. 'I'll go and track down that photographer,' he said.

FaB-Ex '99

1

Bob's efforts had paid off. Between the new marketing strategies, last year's cold-calling, and some clever responses to the world's growing Millennium Bug anxieties, Haywood's was back up to twelve set-ups to complete at FaB-Ex, double the previous year. The company had grown, too, and Bob now had a pool of eight fitters and installers, including Chilly and one apprentice. After a rocky patch the year before, things were looking good now and he had been able to pay each of his guys a decent bonus last Christmas. The whole team of eight were at the NEC for the set-up day this year, and Bob was looking forward to treating them all to a big company dinner that night as a thank-you to everyone.

Chilly had lost a lot of weight, almost certainly on doctor's orders, although Bob suspected that Mrs Chilly was also a driving force behind the transformation. As a result, the skin around his chin and cheeks was droopy, giving him a jowly appearance, and his trousers struggled even harder to stay up. Bob suspected that rather than buy new pairs of trousers with a smaller waist, Chilly had simply punched a few extra holes through his belts. Chilly's visible arse crack had become company legend, and he took a lot of grief for it.

Jamie was still a worry. He and Alison had separated at the end of last year, around the time he was finally coming to terms with the loss of his father. They shared the care for Josh, who was now at pre-school, but the whole situation had changed Jamie. He had become reclusive and distant. As a result, Bob had given him just the one install at FaB-Ex this year, a large stand in the equipment hall. It would take him the whole day, and he would be there on his own. Chilly would check on him every now and then, and Bob too each time he passed by. Jamie had developed a habit of daydreaming, something he hadn't done since his apprentice days.

One major step forward in the business was that Bob had finally given in to pressure and issued mobile phones to each of his senior installers, Chilly, Jamie and Ward. They had become commonplace in the few years before, but Bob had been resistant to getting them, thinking they would be an increased cost that would simply be a distraction for his guys or would be misused. He had one too, and now wished he had bought them for his guys long ago; the ability to contact the fitters on site or for them to relay a message or problem immediately it happened was such a bonus.

He speed-dialled '7', and after three rings Jamie answered.

'Crates there yet?' Bob launched straight into it.

There was a pause, then a noise before Jamie answered, 'Yep, all here, Bob, just starting now.' The answer was curt and to the point, and Bob suspected Jamie was on a downer today. The flipside to him having the phone was that Alison could contact him whenever she wanted and exert pressure on him. Sure enough, Bob heard the beeps on the line that signalled someone was trying to get hold of Jamie.

'I'll let you go then,' Bob replied. 'Call if you need anything.'

'Will do.' It was a hurried response and Jamie hung up quickly. Bob felt for him. He didn't deserve this; he was a good father and was there when he could be, but unfortunately that wasn't as often as either he or Alison wanted. Bob was sympathetic, but ultimately he had a business to run and needed to keep some distance. He put his phone away; he had other priorities today.

He would do a quick tour of all the stands his guys were working on and go to see the girl who had helped him with his flyers the previous year. She had done a superb job and had then arranged five thousand to be printed for him at a lower cost than he had printed five hundred of his original version the year before. He wanted to thank her again.

Once he had done that, he would go and check on Jamie, maybe have a word with him about his situation.

2

It was late lunchtime when Bob arrived at the stand Jamie was supposed to be working on, but there was no sign of him. He looked around the stand. The equipment was all assembled and connected up, but the carpet was messy with tools and stripped cable ends everywhere. That was most unlike Jamie; he was usually very careful with his tools. Left around like this, they could be stolen by anyone walking past. Bob looked around again, but still no sign of him. The area around the stand was hectic, forklifts moving crates and pallets with equipment on, belching out diesel fumes into the path of men carrying boxes and running errands. On the stand opposite, scaffolding had been erected and a man was fitting company lettering to the front of the fascia boards.

Bob picked up the tools and dropped them into the open toolbox before closing the lid and pushing it behind one of the display stands. He pulled out his phone and was about to speed-dial '7' when Jamie walked back onto the stand. He didn't look right and was shocked to see Bob standing there.

'Looking good,' Bob commented, trying to be upbeat and positive. Jamie just nodded but turned his face away. Something was wrong.

'What is it, J?' he asked.

Jamie walked to the back of the stand, looking for somewhere to escape from Bob, but there was nowhere. He put his hands up to his face and rubbed his eyes. Bob caught up with him and pulled his hands away. Jamie had clearly been crying—his eyes were red and puffy, and his cheeks streaked with wet lines.

'What is it, mate?' Bob repeated, gently.

Jamie closed his eyes, the action squeezing out more tears, which raced down his cheeks. He shook his head adamantly, indicating he didn't want to speak. Bob put his arms around the young man's shoulders.

'Oh, mate,' he said, 'what can I do?'

Jamie slumped into Bob, his head buried into the older man's shoulder, and started to sob. 'She's filed for divorce,' he managed between sobs. Bob rubbed his back, struggling himself to hold the tears back. 'And she's taking Josh.'

At this last comment, Jamie started crying again, his broad shoulders moving up and down while Bob patted him on the back. Bob felt his gesture was futile but was at a loss as to what else to do. They were receiving strange looks from the people passing the stand, mostly rough-looking subcontractors and tradesmen, but Bob didn't care.

Eventually, after what seemed an age to Bob, Jamie let go of him and tried to dry his eyes and cheeks on his overalls sleeve, then moved to sit at the back of the stand, the flimsy rear wall moving under his weight. Bob sat down next to him, and the two men remained silent for a couple of minutes, Jamie sniffing periodically and wiping his eyes.

'I'm so sorry, Bob,' Jamie finally said, 'this is the second year I've let you down.'

Bob turned to him sternly. 'Don't you dare—you haven't let anyone down, least of all me. I'm proud of you, proud of the man you've become, and if she chooses to leave you—well then, that's her loss.' He paused, his rant over. 'What do you mean, she's taking Josh?'

'Her father is a divorce lawyer,' Jamie snorted, '... typical, isn't it. She's going to claim I'm unsuitable as a father and that I can't have any more than one visit every two weeks because of the nature of my work. Because I'm never at home.'

Bob didn't answer. He had no experience of this sort of thing and didn't want to get the young man's hopes up. Instead, he changed the subject.

'How much more needs to be done here?'

'Just vacuum the carpet, polish the steel and check the air connection,' Jamie replied.

'Right, I'll get Chilly and the boys to do that, and I'm going to take you home. Go throw some water at your face and freshen up. Meet me at the main entrance in ten minutes. I'll give Mr Winterbottom a call.'

Jamie nodded. 'Thanks, Bob, you sure?'

Bob had already punched Chilly on the speed dial and waved Jamie away. As Jamie left the stand, he heard Bob's voice as Chilly answered.

'Chilly, it's Bob. Can you send Ward over to the Pressto stand? Just needs the air checking and a tidy up ... No, he's not well, I'm going to take him home.' Jamie rounded the corner and disappeared out of Bob's view, as he headed for the toilets to freshen himself up.

Bob hung up the phone, and sighed deeply as he stared in the direction Jamie had gone. His concern for this young man weighed heavy on his mind.

As he dropped the phone back into his pocket, the sales lady from Blue Riband walked onto the stand. She was exactly as Bob remembered her from their meeting the previous year, immaculately turned out and very professional-looking in business attire, with clicky high heels and her brown hair hanging neatly at her shoulders.

'So sorry I missed you earlier,' she said, 'but I was told I would find you here, and I have the latest proofs of your brochures to check over.'

'My dear,' said Bob in a fatherly manner, 'it is not an issue; your colleagues did tell me that you would be back.'

She laughed. 'Yes, like a bad penny, as my dear old grandma would have said.'

FaB-Ex 2000

1

Jamie's year had been a bad one, and he was dreading FaB-Ex this August. A few years ago it was an annual happy time for him, something to look forward to, but not any more. It seemed that if something bad was going to happen in his life, it happened around the time of FaB-Ex. His father's heart attack two years ago, then the divorce bombshell last year ... he wondered if he would get the hat trick this year and what more life could throw at him.

He just had the two stands to fit out this year: he had been allotted Steelfab, which he hadn't done for a few years now, and the Pressto stand, which he had started but not finished the year before. That was fine; he knew what to do and would just knuckle down and get on with it.

Recent improvements in technology allowed the NEC to monitor the demographics of the people attending shows to help with their marketing, but these changes meant he couldn't simply come and go as he pleased due to increased entry and security checks. The NEC checks were so half-hearted, though, that he felt sure he could smuggle a bazooka in, had he wanted to. His lanyard simply described him as 'Subcontractor, Haywood Installations,' but this year it came with a barcode that had to be scanned each time he went in or out. He went through the ritual for the third time that day, but it was the same girl who had scanned him in earlier and she decided not to check his toolbox this time.

Another security breach. He made a mental note to advise any curious terrorists that if they wanted to smuggle a bomb into the show, do it on the third time of entry, inside their toolbox. He smiled at his own dark thought.

As he pushed his way forward into Hall 3, he ended up behind a girl of about the same height as him, with short-cropped brown hair. Could it be ...?

Without thinking, he said, 'Hello, long time no see!'

The girl looked to each side to see if someone was talking to her and then turned round fully. To Jamie's surprise, she was Asian, with dyed hair.

'Sorry, sorry,' he flustered, 'wrong person.' She half-frowned, half-smiled politely, and each moved off in different directions.

The interaction left him wondering what had become of Penny, dear Penny. *She* was something good that had happened at FaB-Ex, though he then reminded himself that they had hooked up four years in a row, disproving his hat trick theory. He wondered again if anything would happen this year at FaB-Ex.

He would start at the Steelfab stand; it would be good to see the guys there again. Had it really been three years since he had seen them and done their install? He wondered if the Charisma Kid was still the same.

As he walked onto the stand, he was met by Bradley, a bit greyer round the temples but still the same old Bradley. He was in jeans and a T-shirt, which Jamie hoped meant he didn't intend to stay and help. Although Bradley could seem quite charming, Jamie knew now that there was another side to him and that he could be insincere and smarmy. Jamie wanted to ask about his son but genuinely didn't know his name, so instead he asked about Don, the sales manager.

'Oh, he's fine,' Bradley answered, 'still with us despite all our efforts to scare him off, and doing a great job.'

'And what about ... err ... what about ...?' Jamie desperately hoped that now he had started down this track, Bradley would help him out.

'Oh, Wallace? He's good too,' Bradley replied, but less enthusiastically. *Wallace*—Jesus, the poor bloke hadn't had too many breaks in life. Jamie smiled again at his own thoughts and managed to disguise it as being pleased that they were both okay. He wondered if there had been a falling out between Bradley and Wallace, as there was no warmth in his father's reply.

'Will they be here this week?' Jamie asked.

'Yes, yes, should be,' Bradley hedged. 'Wallace said he would be here tonight—after all the hard work is done.' Again, Jamie caught an edge to this comment. 'And Don will be here at some point, but he and his wife have just had a baby.'

'Oh, that's lovely,' Jamie enthused. He had liked Don when he had met him.

'Yes, isn't it?' The insincerity was back. 'He met her here at FaB-Ex, you know, a few years ago. Here on our stand, would you believe?' Jamie nodded. 'How about you, Jamie? What have you been up to? We haven't seen you in ages.'

'Not been too good, sir, if I'm honest,' Jamie replied openly. 'My father passed away a couple of years back, and then this last twelve months has been a messy divorce.'

'Oh. I'm sorry to hear that,' Bradley answered awkwardly, looking surprised by so much detail; the Jamie he remembered had been a closed book, very quiet and private.

'Yes, but all over now. Mind you, she took me to the cleaners,' Jamie continued, 'and took my son too.'

Bradley looked uncomfortable and started to glance sideways for a way out of this difficult conversation. Jamie was surprised at himself, too—it must be the medications he was on; they took away the pain of it all but loosened his tongue at the same time.

'Dear, dear, that's no good. Look, I must make a move, so I'll leave you to it.' Bradley shook Jamie's hand and was off the stand very quickly.

2

It had taken Jamie longer than usual to set up the Steelfab stand, even without any interruptions. He found that the medications he was on for his depression took away his keen sense of urgency, so that he tended not to worry about when things would get done. He wasn't allowed to drive on these meds, so he was surprised that Bob was still happy for him to carry out the installation work. He felt sure that if there was an incident, he probably wouldn't be covered by Haywood's insurance, but he didn't really care. At least he had a job and a steady income.

His phone rang; it was Ward, asking how he was doing. With Bob away on holiday in Florida, Chilly and Ward were in charge, and Jamie knew they had been told to check up on him because he was getting calls from them alternately every half hour or so. Under normal circumstances, it would almost certainly have been he and Chilly in charge, but he was happy to take a back seat for the moment. He was struggling to cope with challenging situations and any unexpected stress. He rather curtly told Ward to piss off—something he would normally never do—and pressed the red button to hang up.

He looked around the stand, and then at his watch. Lunchtime, and he was only just finishing here; he still had the Pressto stand to set up. He could feel the panic starting to rise and the dark clouds gathering over him. He looked down; the veins stood out on the backs of his hands. The meds must be wearing off, but he would need a drink to swallow his next dose with and had nothing. If he didn't take the dose soon, that darkness would start to descend.

Jumping to his feet, he checked his overalls pocket for some change and set off for the Piazza. He was feeling bad now for snapping at Ward; the New Zealander was a good guy and would only have been doing what he had been told. He punched Ward's number on the speed dial, but it was engaged, and he left a recorded message to apologise.

The Piazza was heaving, but only with subcontractors. As it wasn't a show day, a lot of the shops and restaurants were closed. He found one that was open and bought a bottle of water and a cheese sandwich. He was stunned at the price and had to rummage around in his pocket for some additional change. Each little incident was stressing him out a bit more, and he could feel the icy talons of paranoia start to grip him. His breath came more quickly now, and there was an urgency to everything he did. He asked for a receipt, which seemed to annoy the man behind the counter. Surely that would be standard practice on a day like this? Again, the panic inched up a notch, and he started to drum his fingers on the counter.

'Come *on*,' he muttered behind gritted teeth. The receipt arrived, and he snatched it away. The man didn't seem to notice and had already nodded to the next customer.

Jamie found a quiet corner under the escalator, away from the mass of people, where he could take his tablet and eat his sandwich. There was an immediate relief in swallowing the tablet, which must be psychosomatic as there was no way it could act that quickly. He took a deep breath and waited for the serenity to return.

He would head for the Pressto stand now and make a start there, but after dropping his rubbish into a nearby bin he felt another panic attack coming on: he wasn't sure which way to head back to Hall 3. He knew this place like the back of his hand, yet he was briefly lost. He had to step back into his quiet alcove by the escalators, out of the flow of people, to allow the feeling to subside. He looked up high around the Piazza for signs to Hall 3—and then he saw her.

She was getting onto the escalator about ten metres away from him, and as she stepped on he lost sight of her. He moved away from the wall to get a clearer view as she passed by, now a couple of metres above him. He stared, open-mouthed, people pushing past both behind and in front of him. He could see her hair, her beautiful hair, and she was wearing a white blouse—it was *her*, definitely her!

'Penny,' he called out, then louder, 'Penny ... *Bad Penny*!'

The girl on the escalator looked round, intrigued by the disturbance beneath her, to see a dark-haired man in blue overalls shouting up at her. Two men on the escalator below her also turned to look at him.

From Jamie's perspective, it seemed to take so long for her to turn her head, as if it was happening in slow motion. Then she just stared at him, before blinking and turning away.

It wasn't her—not even close. Her hair was long, not shoulder-length, and more of a reddish colour, not brown. Her features weren't even similar.

Embarrassed and angry with himself, he looked away and took a deep breath. The few people that were still looking at him turned away; the show was over. Jamie stepped back to the wall, up against the side of the escalator.

'Fuck!' He punched the wall with his fist in anger. *'Fuck it!'*

He was angry that he'd made a scene and even more angry with himself for seeing what was not there. It must be the medication he was on, it *must* be. It might make him feel better about himself but it had stopped him from driving, was losing him his friends and now he was hallucinating, seeing people from his past.

But why *her?*

He picked up his toolbox and headed back for Hall 3. Maybe it's the location—because he was here at the NEC, his mind was reliving events from previous years here.

He felt sure that the quicker he got the job done here and got out, the better.

3

Five hours later Jamie stood on the platform at Birmingham International railway station. His work was done, and it was time to head home. He hadn't wanted to see Ward and Chilly before he left; he just couldn't face them. He simply wasn't good with conversation these days, as it made him anxious, even with people he knew well. He would rather be on his own—but then when he was on his own, his mind wandered and the walls closed in. He was damned if he did, damned if he didn't. In the end he had called Chilly and told him that the two stands were all completed and ready for him to check and have signed off, and that his toolbox was locked away in the Steelfab storage area at the back of the stand.

He looked up at the digital clock just above him as it clicked over to 18:54. The station announcer came over the PA system to say that the next train through was an express and wouldn't stop; would everyone please stand back from the platform edge. No one moved until the train was virtually upon them and a blast from its horn made them jump and step back behind the yellow line.

It was going slowly enough for Jamie to read the stickers on the window stating that it was going to London Euston. He felt his fists start to clench and the pressure rise. *Damn it!* Just his luck, a train to London comes through but he can't get on it.

He remembered what his doctor had told him: if he wanted to come off the medication, he needed to learn to control his anxiety. He lived from one round of tablets to the next, and he had to learn not to. It was five hours since he had taken the last one in the Piazza, three hours until his next, and he could already feel the effects beginning to wear off.

He closed his eyes and took a couple of deep breaths. He had to train himself to do this, to go to his 'happy place', which was Josh. Jamie pictured his little boy, with his happy smiling face, laughing and calling him 'Dada'. It always worked. Jamie could feel himself relaxing, and he opened his eyes. It was still daylight, and another crowd was gathering around him on the platform. There must be another train due. He hoped it would be a stopping train for London.

His doctor had actually told him that he needed to think of *three* happy places and vary between each one he used when he felt the world closing in around him or the darkness descending. This was so that he didn't wear one out. Josh was the obvious first choice; he was nearly four and a half and had started kindergarten recently. Jamie adored him. He was a delightful little boy, and whatever he thought of Alison as a person, she was doing a great job of bringing him up, pretty much on her own.

His second happy place was his childhood Christmases. He pictured his dad hunched over on his bedroom floor in the pitch black on Christmas Eve, quietly trying to assemble a circle of model railway track just by touch. Jamie had woken up and tried to make out what the strange, tortoise-shaped silhouette was in his bedroom. It didn't take long for him to work out what it was, who it was, and what he was doing. Not wanting to ruin the surprise—for his dad more than for him—he had pretended to remain asleep. Then Christmas Day was always a happy day. After presents and a few phone calls, Mum would do a huge roast dinner and then his parents would fall asleep in front of the James Bond film while he played with his new toys. He smiled at the recalled memory, then looked around to make sure no one had seen his brief moment of nostalgia.

He needed a third happy place. He went over his life, thumbing through the various stages of it, trying to recall when he felt most relaxed and carefree, and found himself on the Steelfab stand, falling asleep with his head resting on Penny's shoulder. She was running her fingers through his hair and asking why Chilly was called Chilly. He smiled again, but this time he didn't care if people were watching. It was a happy time, a time he looked back on as exciting and adventurous, but also comforting and reassuring. For a brief second, he felt his anxiety ease and the butterflies in his stomach had gone, the black cloud had lifted; he was back there with her. He had found his third happy place.

The PA system above him once more burst into life, and the lady advised that the next train at his platform would be the stopping train to London, confirming that it stopped at Watford Junction. From there, he could get a taxi home. The thought of getting onto the train was making him edgy, and he tried to remind himself that it didn't involve anyone else and that once on board he could just tuck himself away in a corridor; he didn't need to sit down as that would risk interacting with people. The butterflies were back. His doctor really had been right: it was the big things that had caused his issues, but it was the small things that tipped the balance.

He heard the whir of the electric locomotive as the train pulled into his platform and slowed to a halt in front of him. The crowd around him surged to get on, fighting to get past him, and he just let them go. They wanted seats; he didn't. When a gap appeared, he took it and stepped up into the carriage, but instead of turning left or right for the seats, he walked across to the opposite window and looked out.

Behind him, people were still getting on, some with bags, some briefcases, but virtually all were business people from the nearby NEC and the various conventions and exhibitions taking place there. He turned his back on them and continued to look out of his window.

There was an empty track and then the opposite platform. He heard the station announcer there say that the next train in was the 19:08 to Sheffield, stopping at all stations. The platform had a few people on it but wasn't as busy as his. His eyes settled on a smart-looking woman in a business suit almost directly across from him. She had neat shoulder-length brown hair and seemed to be looking directly at him.

He felt the anger rising once more. Not this again. How many times do I have to think I see her? He decided that it must be because he had just been thinking about her a minute or so before and her image was fresh in his mind, and that once more his brain was playing tricks on him. He turned away, annoyed with himself, and more determined now than ever to do something about these drugs.

On the opposite platform, the woman just happened to be looking at people taking their seats in the train on the opposing platform and had seen him move to the window. She immediately recognised him and missed a breath when their eyes locked for an instant. He was just as she remembered him—his short dark hair, broad shoulders and blue overalls. He turned away just as she raised her hand to wave, and the moment was gone. She thought she saw pain on his face as he looked down, and wondered what was happening in his life. He seemed sad. Was he married, was he heading home to see his kids? At that moment, the Sheffield train flashed past in front of her, snapping her out of her trance and bringing her back to reality.

FaB-Ex '01

1

Bob had managed to secure the spot he had wanted for his own stand. It was directly in front of visitors as they walked through the main doors into Hall 3, the equipment hall. Whether you were a visitor or an exhibitor, you couldn't miss the Haywood Installations stand. It was only small, three metres by three metres, and in fact it was described as a 'booth' rather than a stand, but Bob saw it as the future for his business and was excited about the few days ahead.

Around the walls there were photographs of the installations he and his team had completed around the UK, and on one wall a number of photos of the stands they had assembled and built at FaB-Ex. A team photo took pride of place on the back wall, with Bob in the centre, flanked by Chilly on one side and Jamie and Ward on the other, then the other fitters and apprentices either side of them. All were smiling except Jamie, who had purposely hidden himself behind Ward as the photo was taken and whose face couldn't be seen very clearly.

Bob and Ward had manned the booth on the first two days of the show; Jamie and Chilly had to do it on the last two days, before the big take-down at the end. During these last two days, Bob would wander round the show while Ward headed off to a small refit job on the south coast.

Jamie was able to drive again; he was off his meds and had been given a tentative all-clear from the doctor. In the last twelve months, he had made a concerted effort to control his thinking and to manage life without relying on the prescription drugs. It had been hard work, and he had slipped a couple of times, but he was getting there. Bob was aware that being in front of people at the stand could be the undoing of him, but installs and refits were subjects Jamie knew well. He was hoping that with Chilly's support, this could actually help him to gain confidence—that it would, in fact, bolster his recuperation, rather than set it back. Bob and Chilly had spoken at length about it before the show and reckoned this was a good move. They both wanted the old Jamie back.

Chilly and Jamie arrived together. Although Jamie could now drive, Chilly had driven up and both had been in good spirits on the journey. It was possibly partly nervous energy, as neither was used to being a salesman and, really, that was what Bob was asking them to be for the two days.

'Just tell them what you do,' Bob had said. 'If anyone asks you a question, just answer it, and if you can't, then say you can't but that you'll find out. Other than that, just be your usual bubbly charming selves.'

The old Jamie would have been excited at the prospect; the new Jamie was daunted but trying not to show it. He had his emergency meds in his bag just in case and had agreed with himself that he would use them if he had to, just to get him through these two days.

The pair arrived at the booth early. There was a tall, round table with four stools at the front of the stand and a low table at the rear with tea and coffee-making equipment. A brochure stand in the front corner completed the set-up. It took no more than a minute to take the covers off and fill the stand with Bob's glossy brochures—nothing like the two-plus hours it would take to assemble a stand like Steelfab or Pressto.

It left them with half an hour to kill before the expo day started. Bob went off to fill the kettle while Jamie looked at the photos around the stand. Apparently Bob had struck up a deal with the show photographer to take pictures of specific stands for him, from angles that made them look bigger than they were and with visitors and stand personnel all around them. As an amateur photographer himself, Jamie appreciated how hard this would be to do in the strange, false light of the exhibition halls. He had been trying to get back into his photography, as his doctor had advised him that hobbies were a good idea. He might try to speak to the photographer, or at least watch him to see how he took the shots and what equipment he used.

Chilly returned with the full kettle, plugged it in and turned it on. 'Tea or coffee?' he asked. 'The coffee is that awful cheap sachet shit that you can still taste with your dinner. My recommendation is tea.'

Jamie laughed and nodded. The 'dream team' were back together, and he had a feeling he was going to enjoy today.

With the tea brewing, Chilly joined Jamie looking at the photos. 'Good, aren't they?'

'Really good,' Jamie agreed.

'Apparently he's used them in the brochure too—have you seen them? I'd never tell him, of course, but they do look very professional. He had to get five thousand printed, so we'll still be giving them out in the next Ice Age.'

Jamie laughed again and picked a brochure up off the stand to have a look at while Chilly finished the teas.

The first thing that struck Jamie was the quality of the paper—smooth and somehow luxurious. He looked at the layout and the photos. It really was superb, and Bob had even redesigned the company logo especially for the expo, so that it was no longer the awkward mutation of 'Haywood' that Bob had literally drawn on the back of a cigarette packet.

'I'd buy stuff from us, just based on this alone,' Jamie commented. He turned the flyer over. 'Ooh, double-sided,' he said sarcastically. He recognised all of the photos on the back, as they were up on the booth walls around him—all except one photo right down at the bottom. It showed Bob shaking hands with a young woman, both smiling for the camera. The caption under it read, 'Another happy customer signs off a successful installation ahead of the FaB-Ex show.'

It was the woman who caught Jamie's eye: it was Penny, his dear sweet Penny—slightly more mature than he remembered and dressed in a business suit, but there was no doubt it was her. Jamie caught his breath and his eyes opened wide.

'Chilly,' he said, as calmly as he could, 'who's that?' He pointed at Penny, being careful not to touch the paper where her face was printed.

'Oh, that's the lady who did the flyers for him. She offered to pose with him like that as a mock photo for a successful install. It's a bit of a lie really, because we've never installed their stands, but it looks good. Bob thinks she's the dog's bollocks.'

'What stand is she on?' Jamie asked. His heart was beginning to speed up and he could feel himself beginning to perspire under the shirt.

Chilly screwed his face up in thought. 'Now you're asking,' he said, then jabbed a finger into Jamie's chest. 'Blue Riband, she was on the Blue Riband Catering stand. You know, they were the mob that used to be Wow! but changed their name and company image to get rid of the titties theme—present a more professional face, as it were.'

Jamie was staring at the photo; his eyes hadn't left it. He was searching the woman's features to see if his mind was playing tricks on him again, if there was any chance he could be mistaken—but he was sure it was her.

'Do you know her name?' He asked the question without thinking. He wasn't sure he actually wanted to know her real name; the closest he had come was 'N Dawson', but to him she would always be his Bad Penny.

'Erm, yes, Bob picked up a card when he first met her. Hang on, it'll be in one of these business card folders.'

Jamie was really sweating now. This wasn't his anxiety—he had no cloud over him; this was something different. Quite out of the blue, he was going to discover Penny's real, full name and had the chance to go and find her. *Today.*

Chilly was rummaging around under the table where the kettle was kept, flicking through one of about four books containing Bob's collection of business cards.

'Here she is,' Chilly said. He flexed the clear plastic in the book, freeing the business card and handing it to Jamie. 'I wonder if she was one of them Wow! babes, you know, back in the day? You remember them, short skirts and tits that would 'ave your eye out?' Chilly started laughing at his own comment, and Jamie couldn't help but smile at the imagery.

He held his hand out but couldn't bring himself to take the card. It was almost like handling a precious artefact. This piece of card would demystify Penny; she would become a real person. Chilly dropped it onto the table with a click, like you would a playing card, and Jamie steeled himself to take a look at it.

Sales, Service, Marketing—Blue Riband Catering
And above it, in larger letters,
Natalie Caravello

2

Jamie had kept the card and not returned it to Bob's book. The name kept repeating in his thoughts ... Natalie Caravello ... Natalie ... Nat. In his mind he had built her up as some kind of angel, perfection personified. She represented a happy time to him, a happy time that she was responsible for, but she had then vanished without a real name, just a nickname. Now she was real, she had an identity.

He moved on from her first name to her surname and wondered why it had changed from Dawson to Caravello. There was only one possible reason: she must have got married in the mean time.

He told Chilly he was going to the toilet and left the stand, saying he would be back as quickly as he could so that they could go for some lunch.

What did he have to lose? He had promised himself he would visit the Blue Riband stand at lunchtime, and it was now lunchtime. The morning had been quieter than he had thought, but Chilly said that the mornings were always quiet and it would pick up after lunch. The few people he had spoken to had been very friendly and really interested in what they had to offer. Jamie had to admit that he had enjoyed it. After his initial nerves when the first man approached him, he soon grew in confidence when he described what was and wasn't possible and how he and the Haywood's team could make the lives of the stand personnel much easier. By the time he left the stand, he found he had developed a sales patter and reckoned it sounded good.

Outside the main entry to the hall, he found the map on the wall in its usual place and scanned down until he found 'Blue Riband Catering': Hall 5, J9–12. It sounded like it was a big stand. Pushing past other people looking up stands on the map, he crossed the Piazza and headed for Hall 5. He was genuinely nervous; he hadn't felt like this for many years. Again, it wasn't his anxiety—he had no dark clouds, and he didn't have the feeling that the world was closing in around him. This was genuine excitement, possibly anticipation. Full of bravado, he strode into Hall 5, catching his reflection in a glass door as he did so. He looked sharp.

He found aisle J pretty quickly and began to slow as he walked. J2, J3 ... he felt his nerves getting the better of him, and up ahead he saw a huge open stand reaching up to twice the height of those around it. It was open-plan with green and white tables, chairs and desks spaced out in the centre and more tables, holding sample products and brochures, around the outside.

He suddenly felt very insecure and vulnerable. He couldn't do it. She had clearly gone up in the world, and what had he done? He stopped abruptly, a man walking behind him almost colliding with him. Jamie spun round on the spot, dodged around the man who tutted at him, and headed back the way he had come.

Annoyed with himself, he strode on, head down. Without the pressure of the situation the nerves had gone, but what had he just done? Passing out of the hall, he caught his reflection again in the glass door and stopped.

'For fuck's sake,' he spat out, causing a few of the ushers behind the desk to look up and watch him for a few seconds. He turned round once more on the spot and headed back to stands J9–12. He was a coward, he knew he was a coward, he let people walk over him; but she had never been anything but kind to him, so what was he afraid of?

He walked fast and was back there in seconds, marching onto the stand like he was on a mission.

'Can we help you, sir?' a young man in corporate attire asked him. He could see concern in the man's eyes and realised he must have looked quite angry—only with himself, but it might not have appeared that way.

He adjusted himself, trying to soften his face, and took a breath. It was a simple question, he just needed to ask it.

'Yes,' he stammered, 'thanks.' He could feel his voice cracking with nerves, and hoped it didn't show. 'I'm hoping that you might be able to help me. I'm looking for someone that works for your company.'

'Do you know his name?' the young man asked courteously.

It was the break Jamie needed, and he managed to take another breath. The nerves were easing slightly. *'Her* name, actually,'* he said, 'it's, err ...' He had not said her name out loud before. 'Natalie ... Natalie Caravello.'

The young man twisted his face, then frowned. 'I don't know the name,' he said. 'Let me ask.' He turned to a small group sitting at a nearby table. Jamie hadn't noticed the group before, as they were behind a display screen when he had walked on. He studied them now—was she there? Scanning each head, he only saw men. She wasn't there.

'Hey Dave, you know a Natalie ...' He turned back to Jamie. 'Caravello.'

'Nat?' Dave replied. 'No, sorry mate, she's not with us any more.' He spoke directly to Jamie, who nodded back. That seemed to be the end of it.

If he didn't speak up now, he might not get another chance. 'Any idea where she went?'

Dave, who'd been turning away as Jamie asked, turned back. 'Sorry mate, no, not sure. She left about a year ago, had a baby.'

Jamie nodded back, then thanked the young man for his help and walked off the stand. He felt numb. It wasn't the answer he was expecting, and he wished he hadn't asked. He was distraught and couldn't believe how he felt at being told this. Upset or disappointed? He wasn't sure which, and he just started walking, blind to his surroundings, trying to get his head around this revelation.

FaB-Ex '02

1

It seemed like Groundhog Day. Jamie and Chilly were back in the booth for the second year running. Bob hadn't been sure whether to field Jamie again, but his issues seemed to be levelling out. He was neither good nor bad. The old Jamie wasn't back, but he was an improvement on the Jamie from twelve months ago and seemed to be getting a grip on his health problems, at least outwardly.

This year he had set up three stands the previous day on his own, all completed quickly and signed off immediately. He had been quiet in the evening, just eating his meal, having one drink and then going up to his room, apparently to watch a movie. To the average observer, Jamie just seemed like a quiet, shy man, but both Bob and Chilly knew better. They knew he still wasn't right.

Jamie was actually fighting an inner turmoil. He was desperate not to go back onto his medication—he had so much to lose if he did—but it was hard, so hard to cope without it and appear outwardly like nothing was wrong. He felt like everyone was watching him, judging him, assessing him, trying to work out what his intentions were. In his darkest moments, he was suicidal, but thankfully these were rare. If he felt the world closing in around him and the darkness descending, he would go straight to his happy place: close his eyes and imagine he was with Josh. He saw Josh every second weekend and did his absolute best not to give any hint of his issues, and although Alison probably didn't care, it was a matter of pride that his son didn't see him at a low ebb.

He now only had two happy places; he had had to remove Penny as his third. His memories of her still gave him pleasure, but then he'd remember what he had been told a year ago and his mind would wander to thinking about what could have been. And regrets weren't helpful to him at the moment.

'How's your mum these days?' Chilly asked during a quiet phase in the booth. His question filled a pause but was also quite genuine. He had met Jamie's mother a few times, although it had been some years since he had last seen her. There were a couple of subjects that seemed to bring Jamie out of his doldrums, his mum being one of them, and Chilly knew this from recent experience.

'She's not too bad, thanks, Chill',' Jamie replied. 'Did you know I had to move her into a home earlier this year?'

'No, I didn't. I'm sorry. How's she fitting in?'

'Better than I'd thought, actually. It's a lot less worry for her, there are plenty of activities, and she's made some new friends. Since my dad died she's been pretty much on her own, and although she resisted going there like mad, really wasn't keen, she's now happy she did.'

'There's a bit of a stigma about these places, isn't there? But I think if you can find a good one, they can be really good.'

'You're right,' Jamie enthused. 'Living at home, everything was a hassle for her and I had real concerns. Her osteoporosis is getting bad, and she can't even lift a kettle to make a cup of tea, so I had to buy her a cradle to put it in, so it rocks to pour the water out—otherwise she would almost certainly scald herself.'

Chilly nodded. 'I'm sorry to hear that, but pleased she's making friends again. Give her my best, won't you? Lovely lady.' Then he added, 'Who pays for it?'

'I do,' Jamie replied. 'I'm doing up her house in my spare time, so I can sell it, but in the mean time I'm paying for upkeep for the family home, mortgage on my flat and weekly bills for her place as well.'

'Shit!' Chilly was genuinely surprised. 'I didn't realise.'

'It'll all be okay once I sell the house, but just a bit of a struggle until then.' It was the first time Chilly had heard Jamie say something positive for quite a while.

'You enjoying doing the work?'

'Most of the time,' Jamie confirmed. 'It's just that I don't get much time to do it, and I don't have much spare cash for the expensive bits or the jobs I need to get someone in to do. I reckon I'll be a couple of years yet, finishing it.'

Chilly nodded. Jamie was definitely upbeat about this, and it was nice to hear. 'I'm always happy to help, you know,' he offered, 'within reason, of course. Just let me know, even if you just want some company while you paint.'

Jamie was touched. 'Thanks, Chill', I'll take you up on that.'

It was nearing lunchtime on the first day. Bob had only asked Jamie and Chilly to do the one day this year, after they had spent the previous day setting up stands, and he and Ward would do the rest of the show in the booth before all of them mucked in for the take-down at the end of the week. Take-downs were much quicker and easier than set-ups.

'Want to grab a bite?' Chilly asked. 'You know it'll pick up in an hour or so—this easy life can't go on forever.'

'Good plan,' Jamie answered. 'I'll get my wallet.'

Chilly was delighted to see the spark of enthusiasm in Jamie's manner. It was rare these days. Could this be the old Jamie returning, or was he just covering it up better? Jamie certainly had a lot on his plate, and Chilly knew he wanted to see more of Josh and that Alison didn't make it easy for him.

Jamie unlocked the cupboard under the kettle and rummaged about amongst the business cards and brochures, finally pulling out his wallet. When he turned round, there was a man talking to Chilly, and it took Jamie a moment to place him. It was a face he knew but hadn't seen for a while.

Seeing Jamie standing up and looking at him, the man excused himself from Chilly and walked across to Jamie, offering his hand to shake. 'Jamie, it's great to see you ... I'm Don, I used to work at Steelfab. You used to set our stands up for us—did a great job.'

Jamie had already recognised him and was delighted that Don actually made the effort to speak to him. It was the small acts such as this that helped his inner battle.

'Don, how are you? Did you say "used to" work at Steelfab?'

Don shook Jamie's hand enthusiastically as Chilly joined them. 'I left about three months ago,' Don explained. 'The problem with a small family business like that is that there is simply no room for progression. The family members will always be promoted over you, irrespective of ability.'

Both Jamie and Chilly pictured Bradley and Wallace Copchase in their minds and nodded at the same time.

'Don't get me wrong, Bradley's a good guy, but he will always put Wallace first, and as an outsider I'm the first to be in the wrong. Also, as I'm not his son, I was never privy to the board meetings that were held across the dining room table every night, and of course this is when most of the company policies were decided.'

Chilly cut in. 'I never rated that Wallace. In my opinion, he needs to grow a pair.'

Don laughed but didn't comment. Jamie thought how impressive this was; it would have been very easy to give Wallace a pasting, but he hadn't. Don clearly had integrity.

Don continued, 'The reason I wanted to see you is that my new company are looking at replacing their current installations manager with subcontractors like yourselves, and I wanted to know if you guys—or Bob—would be interested?'

'What about your current installations guy?' Chilly asked, seeing the situation from the perspective of his equivalent.

'He's retiring,' Don explained, 'so we either have to find someone from within the company—and there really isn't anyone—or hire from outside, which will be expensive. At least if we use you guys, we don't have a bloke sitting round in the office between jobs, getting paid for drinking coffee.'

'I reckon Bob would be delighted,' Jamie stated honestly. 'It's the whole reason we're here and have this booth.'

Don seemed relieved. 'That's great.' He started to hunt around in his jacket pocket and pulled out two business cards, handing one to each of the other men. 'Can we set up a meeting with you guys and Bob and get something sorted out? Need to get this up and running in the next couple of months.'

Chilly nodded back at Don and smiled, but Jamie's eyes were fixed on the name on the business card.

Don Caravello
Operations Manager

FaB-Ex '03

1

It had been a good year for Haywood Installations. Bob's decision those few years before to have a FaB-Ex booth of their own to sell their services had been inspired, and the last twelve months had been the busiest yet. Bob had spent a lot of time out of the office in the weeks after the last show, meeting with the various companies that had approached him on the stand. Some had said they would be in touch, others were giving Haywood's a 'trial run', and a couple had actually signed contracts for work to begin immediately. It appeared that the manufacturing industry was picking up, but that small- to medium-sized businesses were nervous of having a full-time installations team in case times got lean again and people had to be either laid off or paid to do nothing.

Initially, this meant that the team at Haywood's was stretched to the limit. Chilly, who had now put weight back on but whose angina seemed to be under control, had become a project manager and would travel from site to site, overseeing the work. This meant that he didn't actually do any heavy lifting or anything stressful, but it also meant that he spent way too much time in his car eating junk food between sites.

Jamie and Ward were the team leaders, and Bob had given both of them pay rises in accordance with their new titles, which pleased them no end. Bob had hired another four young fitters over a six-month period and the company was now twelve strong, the biggest it had ever been. A concerted effort had been made to get every fitter fully qualified and certified to work on-site, so that Bob could move his staff around without it affecting the workload or the finished quality of each installation. It was all coming together.

Ward was now married with a young family and seemed settled and content. Unlike Jamie's ex-wife, Alison, Ward's wife, Diane, didn't seem to mind her husband being away all week. After the Jamie–Alison saga, Bob was very aware of the stresses this can put on a young family, and he had made sure to speak to them as a family, asking Diane to speak to him directly if there was ever an issue.

Jamie was still a concern to Bob. It had been a few years now since Alison had left him, and he still wasn't back to normal. Every now and then the old Jamie would come out for a few minutes before the new, more distant Jamie took over again. His work was first class, and the theory was that his work was his sanctuary. Chilly and Bob had reasoned that he needed his work to forget about his recent past and what he saw as his failures. Bob made sure to allot jobs to him that he knew he would do well and to always keep every second weekend free on Jamie's roster, so that he could see Josh.

Chilly still reckoned that Jamie would come good again and that all it would take would be for him to meet the right girl, but he never did. Bob wasn't so sure. He had witnessed a couple of arguments between Jamie and some of the newer, younger staff, where Jamie had almost had to be pulled off them before it got nasty. Jamie didn't seem to have any patience for the new fitters and couldn't be allowed to train or mentor them—that job fell to Chilly and Ward. Bob wondered if, rather than Jamie's mental health improving, it was actually just the same and he was learning to cover it up better—although a small prod from one of the younger guys and it would all begin to spill out. Was it only just a matter of time before he exploded?

In the few months prior to FaB-Ex, Jamie's mum had taken a turn for the worse, and this concerned Bob too. Apparently she had had a fall at her care home and it had left her with broken bones and some very bad bruising. The physical damage would heal, but she was now scared to go out of her room and refused to be included in any of the scheduled outings. Jamie's two institutions were seeing Josh every second weekend and seeing his mum on the intervening weekends. He seemed to need the routine; it gave his life structure and kept the demons at bay. Bob worried what would happen if either of these routine commitments were taken away.

The one strange thing during the year was that Jamie had requested he not be involved in any of the installations for Don Caravello's new employer, Gloucester Valves. This didn't make any sense, as Jamie had always got on well with Don, and in fact Don had personally asked for Jamie to do some of his tougher installs. Jamie wouldn't give a reason and asked Bob to please respect his wishes. It had left Bob having to make excuses that Jamie was in high demand and was currently on site, on other jobs.

It was Jamie, though, and he was almost family to Bob, who felt he had to do the right thing by him. The younger guys on the team could see that Jamie got special consideration for his manner and behaviour, but they didn't know the history. This year on the stand, Bob had insisted that the younger guys set up the FaB-Ex stands—of which there were fifteen—and the booth would be manned by himself and his management team for the four days of the show. This meant Bob, Chilly, Ward and Jamie had four days together, and all four were looking forward to it.

2

Jamie called his mum a couple of times a day. As with everything else in his life these days, he tended to do it at set times: just after morning coffee to make sure she had had a good night's sleep, and late in the afternoon to check she was going to have her dinner delivered. If he got the chance, he would also call in the evening to wish her goodnight, but with work commitments, this wasn't always possible. However, at the show, he knew he would get the chance.

Today had been Ward's turn to fetch the morning coffees, and Jamie picked up his cup and stepped away from the booth to call his mum. There was a stand opposite that didn't seem to be manned; it just had company literature on racks and large high-quality photos pinned around the walls, so he parked his coffee mug on the unused round table and called her.

As he chatted to her, he watched the Haywood's booth from the opposite side of the walkway and saw Don Caravello approaching. Don enthusiastically shook Bob's hand, then Chilly's and finally Ward's. He must have then asked where Jamie was, as Bob pointed to him, they all turned, and Don smiled and acknowledged Jamie on his phone in the opposite booth. Jamie waved back. He would need to keep his mum talking; he didn't want to have to interact with Don and hoped he would chat with his colleagues for a minute or so, and then move on.

Jamie couldn't explain his attitude towards Don, not even to himself. Don was a great guy, and he clearly had a lot of respect for Jamie and the work he did. They had always got on well in the past. Ever since he had seen that his name was Caravello, the same as Natalie Caravello—his Penny—he had seen this man as everything he had ever wanted to be. Don was charming, friendly, confident, capable, and successful—but to cap it all, he had married the girl whom Jamie had put on a pedestal; he had married his dear sweet Penny. Don had it all, and in his current state of mind, Jamie didn't trust himself.

He knew he was fragile. Every day he battled with himself to keep his head above water. He buried himself in his work and his routines, but if he veered away from these boundaries he would struggle to cope and could be on a short fuse.

His mum was telling him about a game of canasta she had played with her friend Mary and how Mary had definitely cheated, claiming the pack was frozen when it wasn't. Jamie wasn't really listening, but he found the sound of his mum's voice soothing and reassuring. On the stand opposite, Don shook each of the guys' hands once more and waved across to Jamie, who waved back, making sure he was talking as he did, so that Don could see he was busy. The smile from Don was warm and friendly—damn it, he really was a nice guy, Mr Perfect. Jamie said goodbye to his mum and that he would call her this afternoon, then hung up. Checking Don had gone, he crossed the walkway back to the Haywood's booth. Jamie was annoyed with himself for the way he acted, particularly towards Don, who didn't deserve this treatment. But Jamie knew it was a form of self-preservation.

As he reached the booth, Bob put his arm around Jamie and, guiding him carefully, walked away from the booth, onto the carpeted walkway towards the main entry to the hall.

'Now, then,' Bob started, 'we have all four of us been invited out to dinner tonight, by Don Caravello and some of his colleagues from Gloucester Valves.'

Jamie took a deep breath, his mind taking in this scenario that he hadn't anticipated. His peripheral vision began to blur, and he recognised the beginnings of a panic attack. Bob stopped just outside the main entrance to the hall and turned Jamie to face him, immediately seeing that the colour had drained from his face. He looked like he had seen a ghost.

'I don't know what your problem is with Don, he's a true gent; but he specifically asked for all four of us—you included—to be there at the dinner tonight.' Jamie opened his mouth to protest, but Bob got there first. 'I will sit next to you, Chilly on the other side. I don't expect you to be the life and soul of the party, but I want you to be there.'

Jamie closed his mouth and looked down. He trusted Bob. The man knew Jamie had troubles, although he didn't understand them or know of all the causes, but Bob was one of Jamie's rocks. If Bob and Chilly were there, surely he could deal with anything?

Jamie nodded.

'Excellent!' Bob said. 'Apparently a few of their wives will be there too. Don's wife is going. He says she works in marketing for one of the big packaging companies and they have a stand here at the show.'

Jamie's eyes widened, and he struggled to take a breath as panic began to rise. Bob's comment had meant to reassure, but Jamie only felt his personal terrors closing in.

3

Jamie was sweating. He was outside his comfort zone now, but he was going to do this. Going through with this meeting, with this dinner, could perhaps finally put a few of his long-standing demons to bed.

They had closed off the booth a bit early and covered everything up, leaving at about 4.45 pm. The meal was set for 6 pm at a steak house in the city, so they had about an hour before they needed to catch a taxi. Chilly had said he would only take five minutes to freshen up and asked Jamie to meet him in the hotel bar in fifteen minutes. Jamie had jumped at the idea; it gave him an excuse to have a drink for Dutch courage and as a distraction. He suspected Bob had asked Chilly to do this, but maybe that was just his paranoia. He didn't care: he needed a drink and the company of his old friend and mentor.

As he opened the door to the bar, the noise level hit him. The bar was packed. Most people would have come straight from their stands at the show and were now having a drink before dinner. Jamie looked round the bar—mostly men in suits or business shirts, a few women also smartly dressed, but all happy to be knocking back a glass of something after a long day on their feet, selling.

He picked out Chilly's ample frame immediately, sitting right at the bar, with two pints of bitter in front of him. He waved and smiled. Jamie was pleased to see him; tightly packed groups of people like this stressed him out. Chilly patted him on the back as he sat down and handed him his pint. They each raised their glasses and touched in the traditional manner, Jamie noticing that Chilly's was already half-drunk. Jamie took a big mouthful, licked the froth from around his mouth and then took another, before replacing the glass on the counter. He needed that.

He looked at his watch: 5:10. In an hour's time he would see her again - for the first time in ... he had to think about it. Eight years ... nine years? The girl he had put on a plinth, his perfect Penny, had grown up, grown into a woman, got married, had children, and what had he done in that time? He was still doing the same job, for the same people, with the same people. He had a failed marriage behind him and a little boy whom he was allowed to see only once every two weeks. He felt the panic rising and the darkness descending on him, and picked up his glass for another large mouthful of beer.

He guessed he could argue that maybe he had seen her in the interim, but it had turned out to be hallucinations—all in his mind. His breathing started to pick up and he could feel his chest tighten as he thought about her. Did she know he was coming? Would she even remember him?

'So, how's your mum?' Chilly asked, cutting into Jamie's train of thought and saving him from himself.

'She's fine,' Jamie answered, 'she's worried that she got diddled at canasta.'

'Well, if that's the worst of her troubles, then life can't be too bad, can it?' Chilly answered.

Jamie felt his mind wandering back and reached for his pint glass again, his security blanket. A thought struck him as he did so: was he turning to alcohol in his time of need? *Oh bugger, he was going to become an alcoholic as well!* He took a large mouthful all the same as Chilly continued.

'What about you—how are you?'

The question surprised Jamie. It was unlike Chilly, but the older man was looking him directly in the eyes, unblinking. Jamie felt he was reading his mind and had to look away.

'I'm fine.'

'No, you're not.' Chilly's answer was immediate and sharp. 'You're not okay. I watch you at work and I watch you here at the shows, and you're not okay—but I don't know why.'

Jamie looked back up at him, Chilly was still looking him directly in the eyes.

'I worry about you, mate,' he continued, ' and I want to help, but I don't know what I can do.' He paused for a sip of beer, while Jamie sat open-mouthed. 'You're a smart young man, intelligent, capable and likeable. You're free and single with a lovely little boy who adores you. You have your life in front of you, and what are you doing with it?' Jamie didn't answer. 'Eh?' Chilly prompted.

Jamie still didn't answer—he didn't know what to say. Chilly carried on.

'You have a good job, you've not long had a promotion and a pay rise, and you're well respected for the work you do. Life's good, mate. When are you going to realise that?'

Jamie nodded. He knew Chilly was right; he knew his problems all stemmed from himself.

Chilly attracted the barman's attention and ordered two more pints of bitter.

'Now push that first pint away ...' Jamie looked at him questioningly. 'Go on, push it away, you don't need it anymore.' The glass had about one mouthful left in it, but Jamie did as he was told and pushed it away, just as a fresh pint was placed on the counter in front of him.

'Now listen to Uncle Chill',' Chilly said, now with a smile on his face. 'That last pint represents your life up until now, and you are going to push it to one side, forget about it.' He slapped Jamie on the arm as he was speaking. 'This fresh pint represents your new life—from this second onwards—okay?'

Jamie smiled and nodded as he listened to this apparently wise old sage.

'I want to see you recognising yourself for what you are, and for what you will be—okay?' For the second time, Chilly prompted Jamie, but this time he wanted a response.

'Yes,' he answered quietly.

'Louder!' Chilly demanded. '"Yes, Chilly."'

Jamie smiled and raised his glass, the two receptacles touching with a clink. 'Yes, Chilly,' he answered, louder.

Chilly was right: what was he down about? He needed to hold his head up high. He had a good job and was surrounded by good people; he had a son he was proud of; and whatever had caused his self-doubt was now all behind him.

He took a big mouthful of beer, as did Chilly, who raised his glass in front of him.

'Good,' he said, 'here's to the new Jamie.'

Jamie thought about what he had coming up that evening. Chilly was right: what did he have to worry about? He *did* have a good job, and he *had* been promoted recently. Surely the fact that he was still with the same company was something to be proud of, because it showed loyalty and integrity? He nodded to himself. And what about her—what about his Penny? She had moved on, they had very different lives now, there was no reason to be concerned or worried about meeting her. Hell, she might not even recognise him—and if she did, so what?

Jamie took a deep breath and looked across at Chilly, who seemed to be having a coughing fit. He must have taken too big a mouthful, or it had gone down the wrong way.

'You all right, Chill'?' Jamie slapped him on the back, but Chilly fell forward onto the bar, his left arm knocking over his fresh pint of beer, which tipped over both men's trousers.

'Chilly!' Jamie shouted, jumping to his feet. Chilly managed to look round at him, but his arms and legs seemed to be out of control and had gone loose and floppy. Jamie tried to catch him as he fell from his bar stool. Chilly was a big man, but Jamie was strong and with both hands under his armpits, managed to pull him up and propped him back on the seat.

Chilly was wheezing now, and the scene had attracted attention in the bar. The barman was right in front of them across the bar, looking very concerned. Chilly looked up at Jamie, his eyes bloodshot and his lips a grey-blue.

'Oh shit, Chilly, no!' He turned to the young barman, watching in horror. 'Call an ambulance!'

The young barman didn't move, frozen to the spot, watching the scene in front of him.

"*Now!*' Jamie screamed.

4

Jamie sat in the corridor, waiting to be told what was happening. He hated hospitals. He had been very lucky in his life to have spent very little time in them. He had been allowed to ride in the ambulance with Chilly from the hotel bar to the hospital, but as soon as they had arrived it was as if the medical services had switched up a gear. Chilly had disappeared on his wheeled stretcher, surrounded by medical staff, while Jamie had tried to follow on foot and had lost him along the way. He eventually found the Coronary Care Unit, where he was told that Chilly had had a heart attack, but that they could give him no more details 'at this time'.

Everything around him was pale-coloured, white or a clinical grey-blue. There was a smell of disinfectant and a sound of beeping machines. It was the sound, smell and colours of pain, maybe even of death. Nothing in his perception even remotely represented good news in any way. Still, he waited, hoping for an update on his friend, his colleague, his mentor, his Chilly. He couldn't lose him.

He looked at his watch; it was 7 pm. Somewhere in the centre of the city, Bob and Ward were having dinner with Don and his wife and their colleagues. Bob had messaged Jamie a couple of times to ask where he was and why he wasn't at the restaurant. Jamie had thought of answering, but what would he say? There was nothing that Bob could do. If Jamie told him what had happened, Bob would come running to the hospital, but what good would that serve? He would miss the dinner with the guys from Gloucester Valves just to sit in a corridor with Jamie, waiting for an update. It would serve no purpose, so Jamie didn't answer and sat there on his own.

Jamie thought about Penny. She would be there too, perfect in every way, but oblivious to the man in the hospital who could not stop thinking about her. It was nine years since he had last seen her, but he couldn't get her out of his mind.

It didn't matter. What mattered now was Chilly. Jamie felt the panic rising again within him, the same panic he had felt when he had been told that Alison was leaving him, that his father had died, and that he could only see Josh once every two weeks. Chilly had to be okay, he just had to be.

Jamie's mind was a whirl. Had anyone contacted Chilly's wife, Gayle? He doubted it. Jamie pulled out his phone, toggled down his contacts list until he reached 'Chilly—Home,' and pressed the green 'Dial' button.

He took a deep breath as Gayle Winterbottom answered at the other end.

FaB-Ex '04

1

'It's been a real mixed bag this year,' Bob told her with a heavy heart. 'On the one hand, business is booming—we've never been busier. Work is coming in faster than we can deal with it, and we've had to recruit additional staff and then subcontract out. Don't get me wrong, it's a great problem to have ...'

'And what was the flip side?' she asked. 'You said it's been a mixed bag?'

Bob sighed and looked away, creases appearing on his forehead as he chose his words. 'I lost two of my longer-term staff,' he said, 'who were almost like family.'

They were both sitting on tall stools at the high round table in the Haywood's booth. The booth was in its now-regular spot, just inside the main entry to Hall 3, the equipment hall. Ward appeared with a cardboard tray of takeaway coffees, pulled two out of their recesses and placed them carefully on the table in front of them, smiling at each in turn. They both thanked him.

'Anyway,' Bob continued, 'enough of our company history, you don't need to know this. Let's crack on with the flyer revamp, I'm quite excited to see it.'

'No, tell me, Bob,' she insisted, 'I'm interested. Please tell me what happened?'

Bob sighed and caught Ward's eye accidentally. Ward looked away and stepped out of earshot, knowing his presence might inhibit Bob from perhaps bending the truth a little for the sake of a relative stranger.

'One of my guys had a heart attack this time last year,' he started. 'Rushed to hospital and is no longer with us. He was my main man—he'd been with me since I started the company fifteen years ago ... he was like a younger brother. The sort of person you both curse and admire in equal amounts. The best worker you could imagine, and really old-school—plenty of common sense, a great attitude, and technically competent—but best of all was how he treated the younger guys. They all looked up to him and he was a great role model. We all miss him.'

There was a pause while Bob reflected on what he had just said, and he thought of Chilly and how he should be here with them on the stand.

'And the other?'

'Hmm?' Bob prompted.

'You said there were two of them—that you'd lost.'

'Oh, yes.' Bob had forgotten his train of thought, and dismissing Chilly, he moved on to Jamie. 'My fitter, who was with him when he had his heart attack—went with him in the ambulance, witnessed it all—he then had some sort of nervous breakdown. The two of them had always been close, and the poor guy took it really badly. He'd been treated in recent years for anxiety after his marriage break-up, but he seemed to be doing okay until the heart attack incident, and then he seemed to just go to pieces.'

'That's really sad,' she said. 'It sounds like he'd had a troubled few years?'

'Well, that wasn't the end of it. About a month later, his mum passed away. It wasn't unexpected—she'd been getting quite frail—but it was probably the final straw. He's an only child, and now all the people he was closest to were gone.'

The woman nodded. 'We forced him to take a few weeks off work; you know, come back when he was ready. The problem was that he needed work, he needed the routine and the distraction. On his own at home he had too much time to think and wallow in his own misery, and he begged me to let him come back, which I did. Well, I thought to myself, "what harm could it do?"'

Bob sighed and looked her in the eyes. 'Then about a week after he had come back, he was doing a big job on site for the guys at Steelfab—'

'Ah yes,' she said, 'I know Steelfab.'

'Well, he was on-site up in Liverpool, with the younger bloke—Wallace, the boss's son ...'

She nodded again. 'I've met Wallace,' she said, and the two of them exchanged a knowing glance.

'Wallace complained to his father about something Jamie had done—or hadn't done, I can't remember—instead of broaching the subject directly with Jamie. Jamie called him a sneak, or a snake?—again, I can't remember. So Wallace complained to Daddy. Jamie saw red, punched him once on the chin, once in the guts, kneed him in the bollocks and finally landed a perfect right hook on his nose, breaking it completely and knocking Wallace unconscious.'

The woman started to giggle. 'No, really? Poor Wallace!' then started smirking again and made a show of covering her mouth while she laughed behind it.

'Look, I'm not saying Wallace didn't deserve it—he is two-faced—but Jamie simply shouldn't have done what he did. It was terrible.'

'So what happened then?'

'Wallace's father, the MD, Bradley—he wanted to sue us for all we had, but we managed to settle out of court as long as I paid for all damages, all legal costs and all of Wallace's medical bills —which I'm told included for two new front teeth and a complete nose reconstruction.'

She started giggling again as she pictured Wallace with two teeth missing and splints running down his nose.

'What about your employee?' she asked. 'What happened there? What became of him?'

'I had to fire him on the spot. I had no choice; he was a liability. Of course, as soon as I did that, he had a full-on breakdown and had to be taken into care, suicide watch and everything ... he was a mess. In his eyes he had no friends, no family, no marriage and now no job. But what else could I do?'

She nodded sympathetically. 'Poor guy. Have you seen him since? Is he okay now?'

'I know where he is, but no, I haven't seen him. He's undergoing that ECT shock therapy treatment at the moment.' She shook her head; the acronym meant nothing. 'Electro-something-therapy, I can't remember what it stands for—but it's where they attach electrodes to you and pass current through your brain. Apparently if done correctly it can work wonders, sort of re-sets the brain, reboots it like a computer—so, fingers crossed. He's on what they call an acute course, used on the worst of the worst—you know, the depressives, the psychotics and the suicidals.' Bob looked sad, his eyes cast down to the floor.

'Sorry,' she said, putting her hand on his arm, 'I shouldn't have asked.' Surprised, he looked up at her. She had kind eyes and an understanding manner.

Bob pulled his arm away and wiped his nose. 'No, it's fine. He was such a good kid, and he grew into one of the finest young men I've known, but he was always a sensitive lad, and the chain of circumstances was just too much for him. Hopefully this shock therapy stuff will work, but we'll see.' He sighed and looked up at her again. 'Enough of this, let's have a look at these new flyers you've done,' he said, adding, 'Have you changed your hair? It looks different.'

She smiled as she pulled the printed samples of the Haywood's flyers out of her leather wallet.

'Yes, I have, actually,' she said, clearly impressed that he had noticed. 'I've gone strawberry-blonde. I did it a few years ago and always liked it, so I thought I'd try it again.'

'Well, it suits you,' Bob confirmed, taking the first flyer from her, and turning it over in his hand.

FaB-Ex '05

1

'Are you sure you want to do this, Bob?' Ward asked.

'Certain,' Bob answered emphatically as they walked along the blue-carpeted walkway towards the Steelfab stand. 'It's been over a year now since the ... err, incident with Jamie and Wallace. We should make amends, smooth things over.'

Bob was walking with purpose, striding forward, on a mission. Ward suspected he was actually nervous but possibly felt it was something he had to do, like ripping off a plaster.

On the Steelfab stand, the only person in sight was Bradley, who was pretending that he was on the phone and that he hadn't seen them walking towards him. Bob noticed that Bradley had one of the latest mobile phones; the Copchases were always among the first to get their hands on new technology so that they could show off.

Bob led the way, veering off the main walkway and onto the green carpet of the Steelfab stand. Ward followed him and couldn't help but look at the assembly workmanship of the equipment on show. For obvious reasons, Haywood's were no longer doing the Steelfab installation, and it showed. He saw cable ties strapping power cables to supports, and there were unsightly marks on the stainless steel. He resisted the temptation to pull a face or to go across and wipe the marks off, which was an occupational habit.

'Bradley!' Bob walked up to him, offering a hand to shake, a truce. Bradley hung up from his apparent phone call, popped his phone on the table, and did his best to make out it was the first time he had seen Bob. He was a poor actor and Ward, following behind now, couldn't help but smile. Bradley mistakenly took his smile as a friendly gesture and tentatively shook both their hands tentatively.

'Gentlemen,' Bradley replied, 'where's your ... err ... colleague, Jamie?'

'No longer with the company,' Bob waded straight in. 'We had to let him go.' Both Ward and Bob looked away as he said this; the whole affair was still a bit raw for them.

Bob expected a retort from Bradley, but all he said was, 'I understand. It was an ugly scene; I have no doubt that it must have been very embarrassing for you.'

What could Bob say? He couldn't disagree. 'Yes, it was. And we have a long history, you and I'—he looked Bradley in the eye—'so I wanted to come and apologise to you personally, to show there are no hard feelings.' He offered his hand again, and Bradley took it. This was actually going a lot better than Bob had anticipated.

Behind him, Ward stood motionless, listening to the interaction, like Bob's bodyguard. He had said to Bob as they had walked over that he would have paid money to see Jamie bring Wallace to the floor, clutching his groin with one hand and feeling for his missing teeth with the other. They had both laughed and Bob had agreed that he would have, too: quite a lot of money, in fact. Ward smiled again as the image came back to his mind, and he caught Bradley's eye, who once again took it as a smile of friendship.

'Where is Wallace?' Bob asked. 'Is he around? We owe him an apology, too.'

'Gone for coffees,' Bradley answered, 'just a few seconds ago. If you chase him, you'll catch him up.'

Relieved at an excuse to end what would otherwise be a potentially difficult conversation, Bob agreed to follow young Wallace towards the coffee shop and have a word with him there. He and Bradley shook hands for the third time and awkwardly agreed to talk again after a discreet period about using Haywood's services once more. Pleased with the outcome, Bob and Ward waved themselves off the green carpet. Ward looked back to see what appeared to be a very relieved Bradley watch them leave.

'One down, one to go,' Bob said. 'Now let's go find that wanker of a son of his.'

'Apologising to him is going to hurt,' Ward commented.

'Got to do it, though. It's the right thing to do.'

2

'Have you heard any updates on Jamie recently?' Ward asked as he and Bob walked along the main walkway carpet towards the main coffee shop.

'Nothing for a year now,' Bob replied.

Unlike the journey to the Steelfab stand, Ward noticed that their pace was extremely slow. Apologising to Bradley was something Bob knew he had to do as a professional, but apologising to Wallace would really go against the grain.

'I lie awake at night and think about him, Ward,' he continued. 'I feel so badly for the poor kid.'

'Not a kid any more.'

'I know, but when I took him on all those years ago he *was* just a kid. He was so positive, so upbeat, keen to please and do a good job. He became almost like family. They do say never to employ friends or family, don't they?'

'So how did it come to this?' Ward was genuinely interested. He had joined the company when Jamie was already a quiet recluse and had assumed he had always been like that. He'd only rarely seen glimpses of this upbeat, happy young man that Bob would describe.

'I don't know. Perhaps he always had it in him, and it took his series of bad luck incidents to bring it out. What do they say? Still waters run deep. Whatever ... I feel responsible.'

'Well, you shouldn't, Bob. How could it be in any way your fault? Anyway, if you ask me, he did us all a favour.'

They were approaching the coffee shop and there was a line of people in a queue outside, waiting to order their mid-morning pick-me-up. This was always a busy time for coffee sales, and it struck Bob that if he did have to apologise to Wallace, he really didn't want to do it in such a public place. He hadn't thought this through, and now regretted this move.

At the end of the queue, next ahead of them in the line, was the unmistakable profile of Wallace Copchase. Bob spotted him first and held a forefinger to pursed lips to indicate to Ward to change the subject. Wallace was talking to another man around the same age as they approached, and he hadn't seen them, as his head was turned slightly away. His monotone voice was unique, and Bob mused that had he not been Bradley's son, he would probably be working in a backroom somewhere, safely distant from any possible interactions with the general public.

Bob noticed also that Wallace's hair was thinning, like his father's, and he could see a shiny scalp beneath the sparse coverage above his forehead. He also had quite a tan; must have been away on holiday recently—the Copchases seemed to like the Caribbean. In fact, he wondered if Bradley might actually own a holiday villa out that way somewhere.

Wallace was still talking to the other man but, aware of two people joining the queue behind him, had turned away so that his back was facing them.

'He was clearly mental,' Bob and Ward overhead Wallace say, 'just snapped, lost his mind.' The other man nodded the way people do when stuck in a conversation not by their own choice. 'Mind you, he was crap at whatever he did. He couldn't hold his marriage together either, lost his kid apparently, and of course they had to fire him from work.'

Bob perked up, Ward too. Was Wallace talking about the incident with Jamie a year or two ago?

'So what happened—did this all take place on-site, in front of a customer?' the man asked Wallace.

'On-site in Liverpool. It was embarrassing,' Wallace continued. Bob and Ward had tuned in closely now, and even though the metallic-sounding voice annoyed them, they couldn't stop listening. 'He was doing a crap job for us, and I told him so, and he just snapped—just totally lost his shit, in front of everyone there.'

Ward was tensing up and looked across at Bob, who was turning red, clearly bristling.

'He had a go at me, but I got the better of him—flattened him with one blow,' Wallace continued. 'That company had always done a crap job for us, but he was the worst.'

That was it.

Bob couldn't listen to any more and, drawing a deep breath, he grabbed Wallace by the shoulder and spun him round. Wallace was stunned to see Bob's face millimetres from his own, eyes bulging and a vein in his forehead ready to pop.

'Oh, hello, Mr Haywood. How nice to see you.' Wallace didn't miss a beat.

Sensing trouble, Wallace's conversation partner took the opportunity to turn away and made his escape, leaving the three men in a close huddle.

'You are a worm of a man,' Bob hissed. 'How *dare* you?' He began to jab Wallace in the chest from close range as he spoke the words - one jab per syllable.

'Bob, leave it, he's not worth it.' Ward tried his best to defuse the situation.

'You're right, mate.' Bob didn't look away, his eyes fixed on Wallace's as he answered Ward. 'He's not worth it. Jamie was worth a hundred of him. He knows damn well that he always did a good job with his poxy set-ups ... *always*!' The last word got Wallace two more jabs in the chest, but Bob hadn't finished and, if anything, was working himself up into quite a rage.

'You didn't knock him down; he had you on the floor weeping like a baby—like the coward that you are!' More jabbing in the chest, which caused Wallace to step backwards. 'You didn't tell him he was doing a crap job; you went crying to Daddy instead of handling it yourself!'

Wallace continued stepping backwards, Bob moving forward, keeping the same distance from him and still jabbing him in the chest. Ward stood still, watching as Bob unleashed his growing anger. He knew he had to do something to stop this—Bob was creating a scene and drawing a crowd.

'What's going on here?'

Ward looked round to see Don Caravello walk up to him from the coffee shop with a hot takeaway cup in his hand.

'I'm going to have to pull Bob off him,' Ward explained. 'We just overhead Mini-Me telling someone how Jamie always did a crap job and how Wallace gave him a beating, then he started slagging off Haywood's as a company.'

'Oh dear,' Don started to laugh, 'that wouldn't go down well.'

The two men watched as Bob kept jabbing Wallace in the chest. Wallace looked round for help, but no one seemed to want to assist. Bob was swearing now—Ward could hear the f-word in frequent use and was now worried that Bob would completely overstep the mark, just as Jamie had done a few years before.

'We'd better stop this,' Don said, 'much as I'm enjoying it. I so wish I had been there when Jamie gave this little shit his beating. I can assure you I wouldn't have stepped in then—it would have been one of the most gratifying things I have ever seen. But we do have to stop Bob here and now.'

Both men stepped forward to try to separate Bob from Wallace. Wallace, seeing his ex-colleague Don and Bob's colleague Ward walking towards him, backed away even more quickly, not realising that there was a low bench behind him. His calves hit the bench and stopped, but his momentum took him over the back of it and he fell onto the carpet. The three men approaching Wallace all stopped and watched as he tried to squirm away from the bench and escape across the floor. As he did so, a spreading stain appeared on the front of his trousers and became more obvious as the seconds passed.

Don nobly stepped forward, swapped his coffee cup to his right hand and offered Wallace his left to pull him up. Beyond his embarrassment, Wallace looked relieved.

'Thank you, Don.' He looked across at Bob, who had stopped ranting when Wallace had fallen over backwards, and gave him a look as if to say 'go to hell'.

Don made a play to try to pull Wallace to his feet, avoiding the growing pool of urine on the carpet in front of him. It appeared Wallace was simply too heavy to pull up, and Don had to use his other hand as well. He brought his right hand across to help pull Wallace up but squeezed the plastic coffee cup in the process. It exploded in his hand and in front of him, pouring hot coffee all over the already compromised Wallace, who yelped in pain as the hot liquid went all over his face, arms and chest.

'Ah, sorry, mate,' Don said calmly, the tone in his voice confirming that it was no accident. He let go of Wallace who fell back onto the carpet. 'At least the piss stain on your trousers blends in now.'

Wallace was close to tears as he looked from side to side for someone else to help him, but still no one came forward. The group of people watching had grown from just those in the queue and was now at least thirty strong. Don, completely unfazed at being the centre of attention, turned to one side and dropped the now-empty coffee cup into a wire-mesh bin, then shook his hands to get rid of the excess coffee. He shrugged his shoulders at Bob and Ward.

'I'll come see you on your stand,' he said and calmly walked off as if nothing had happened.

Ward knew that they too had to leave; they didn't need to be a part of this any more. He put his arm around Bob's shoulders and guided him away from the scene and off along the blue carpet. Bob couldn't take his eyes off Wallace, still lying on the ground, his legs and feet hooked over the bench.

'Eyes forward, Robert,' Ward said, as he physically turned Bob's head away, 'nothing more to see here.'

FaB-Ex '06

1

Jamie wasn't sure quite how he felt walking back into FaB-Ex. There was the feeling of familiarity—it was a place and surroundings that he knew well, the noise and smell of the forklifts buzzing around with crates and pallets, the fitters and subcontractors all trying to get their jobs done as quickly as they could. But FaB-Ex also held memories for Jamie, and they were a mix of good and bad.

The ECT shock therapy seemed to be working for him. Jamie had accepted that it would be a long haul, but he was prepared for it and it had now become part of his routine. He needed routine: it meant he had no surprises, and he still struggled to cope with surprises. He had been told that he might have some memory loss, particularly his long-term memory, and this concerned him. There were some things he would be happy to forget, but there was a lot that he was desperate to hang on to.

He did an exercise in his own mind where he tried to recall every birthday and Christmas with Josh—he couldn't lose those. He would run through Josh's first Christmas, then his first birthday, and then each one after that in order. So far, so good; they were all there and in sequence. Once in a while, if he lost concentration, he would find himself struggling to recall one of the more recent birthdays, and then the panic would start to rise.

FaB-Ex was a different matter. He had been doing this exhibition for so long that he knew the NEC, particularly these three halls, so well. The familiarity brought him confidence, but it also reminded him of Wallace, of Chilly's heart attack, and of the time he had lost his temper with that amazing girl he had met. He still thought of her as his Bad Penny, but she had gone on to marry the guy from Steelfab ... Don. His mind ran in circles as he thought, jumping from person to incident to memory and back again.

He thought of Bob and Chilly and how kind they had been to him, and of the guys from Steelfab and the other companies he had worked for, but that reminded him of how he had beaten up Wallace, and he felt a twinge of regret and embarrassment. His face creased up at the thought. His mind moved to the earlier years when he and Chilly used to set up together and have such a good laugh. He remembered the first one-night-stand with Penny and their subsequent meetings—at least he still had those memories. The creases on his face changed to a smile.

And here he was, back again ... back at the NEC, back at FaB-Ex. He took a deep breath as he walked through the main entry doors and flashed his subcontractor's badge at Security. It was early, and he was surprised there was anyone at this time to check the badges. As he walked through into Hall 3, it was like he had never left; it was all just as he remembered it. And it was bustling. Obviously the other subcontractors had had the same idea and were also in early to make a start. Jamie knew where he had to go and what he had to do, and if he cracked on with it, he could be all done before the regular stand attendees arrived for the day. It was unusual to do the full set-up for a stand on the morning of Day 1, and risky too, but as it was simply a case of unpacking crates, Jamie wasn't in the least concerned.

He had been with his new company around eight months now and was still on probation. He had another four months to complete, and if he kept his nose clean then he would join their payroll as a regular fitter-installer. The operations manager would be in at 10 am and either approve or disapprove his work. Jamie's plan was to be nearby but out of the hall at that time, and he would do his best to ensure that everything was perfect. His new employer was a German company that was trying to break into the British market. They were very different to Bob and Chilly to work for: there was no room for error, and the work environment wasn't considered a place for fun—it was a place where there was a job to be done.

This suited Jamie just fine; it meant he could do his job and do it well, then move on to the next job, with minimum interaction with the customer or with his colleagues. So far, he had been praised for his work; in fact, his attention to detail had been commented on a number of times.

He felt he was finally winning the battle; perhaps his life was getting back on track. He had a new job, a source of income, and a potential future. He had had to agree to the extended probationary period due to his past and his ongoing medical treatment. His new company seemed to be confident in his work ethic and his abilities but had concerns over his character. He understood; if he were in their shoes, he would quite rightly have concerns, too.

His life had changed in other areas as well. His ex-wife, Alison, had found someone else and was soon to be remarried, which would help him financially. Jamie had met her fiancé, David, who seemed a nice guy; he didn't really care except that whoever she ended up with would obviously be a big influence on Josh. Coming from a big family, David was great with kids and didn't appear to have any airs or graces. In fact, he and Jamie had got along well each time they had met. Alison, too, had changed since she had met David—she was softer, less demanding on Jamie and more tolerant of him wanting to see Josh. Jamie had to admit that David was clearly more suited to Alison than he had ever been; he brought out the best in her, something he had always struggled to do.

Jamie smiled as he thought of Josh, who was his main happy place now. Alison had continued to be a good mother to him, as Jamie hadn't been around as much as he would have liked to be, nor been as much of an influence on him as he would have hoped. Josh was polite and respectful and was doing well at school. Jamie was really proud of him.

He arrived at the stand with the company's name, 'Norbert Baumgarten', stencilled onto the white tag that stuck out into the walkway. It was a big stand and would take some filling, but there was no heavy equipment and nothing to wire up, mainly tables and chairs, plus a few sales samples. At the moment, all that was there was the carpet and six large wooden crates. Jamie wasn't fazed; he had three to four hours and knew what he was doing. He placed his toolbox against the back wall and cracked his knuckles in preparation.

2

Jamie looked at his watch: 9.45 am, perfect timing. The ops manager said he would be here at 10 am—and knowing him, it would be exactly at 10 am.

He looked around the stand. The now-empty crates were all stacked at one end and the demo samples, tables and chairs were laid out exactly to the plan he had been given. He had even managed to vacuum the carpet. It looked really good, and he was pleased with his work.

He closed the lid of his toolbox, picked it up and left the stand. It was even busier now—as well as all the subcontractors, the hall was beginning to fill with stand personnel getting ready for Day 1. Jamie was beginning to feel a sense of oppression, as the risk of bumping into people he knew increased as time passed. He was nervous that either he might not remember them and would appear rude, or they wouldn't be the people he would wish to bump into.

However, he had one more stop before he left the hall, and he headed for the main entrance. Approaching it slowly, he made his way towards a small booth close to the entry point and picked out the sign that said 'Haywood Installations'. It was Bob's usual three-metre by three-metre booth, and he could see at a glance that there was no one there. If Bob was here, and if Ward still worked for him, they would be on their way here now from the hotel, so he probably only had a minute or two. This would only take a second, and he walked into the booth, aware of the flood of people moving past him.

Again, Jamie took a deep breath as he looked around the small stand. This time it wasn't because he was anxious, it was another sensation—possibly nostalgia or something similar. There was a high table and some stools, but the focus of the stand was all the photographs around the walls.

One by one, he looked at each of the photos. A lot were of completed site installations or satisfied customers shaking Bob's hand. He reached a section entitled 'Our Story', which had a brief write-up on the history of Haywood Installations, surrounded by group photos. The top photo was a head-and-shoulders of Bob Haywood, probably taken recently; he was looking older but more distinguished. Jamie smiled and resisted the urge to touch his face. To one side there was a photo of the early team, with Bob, Jamie, Chilly and that early apprentice he took on, the one who left as soon as he had qualified ... was it Craig? The photo was taken in front of their offices, and Jamie suspected it had been included as it was probably the only photo taken of Bob's team in the first few years. He looked at Chilly—dear old Chilly, how he missed him. It was too much, Jamie felt himself welling up and had to look away.

Crouching, he turned to the photo on the other side of the write-up and winced again. It was the same picture used on the back of the early Haywood's brochure and showed Bob shaking hands with a well-dressed lady—but not just any lady. It was Penny, his dear sweet Penny.

It was too much for Jamie and he turned away, picked up his toolbox and almost ran off the stand. He had wanted to look at the photos in the hope they would bring back some happy memories for him—and they had. But the memories represented a life long gone, a life he had lost forever.

He wiped a tear from his eye as he pushed his way forcefully through the throng of people heading in the opposite direction into the packed hall.

3

'Who would do this,' Ward asked, 'and why?'

He and Bob stood with their hands on their hips, surveying the Haywood's stand.

'I don't know,' Bob answered curtly, 'but I'm damn well going to find out.'

The exhibition had started. Around them, people flooded into the hall, mostly stand staff running late but also the first show attendees, hoping to make an early start. Bob and Ward had arrived late too, but only by a few minutes; the booth was already set up and the first morning was always slow, so they hadn't been in a rush.

However, when they arrived at the stand, they were horrified to find the table and stools lying on the floor, brochures strewn everywhere, and all the posters and photos on the walls torn down the middle. Thankfully, Bob always had spares of the posters and photos and was in the process of finding them while Ward pulled the remains of the old ones down and picked up all the brochures.

'Rival company?' Ward continued, ignoring the tone in Bob's voice. 'Or are you thinking it was that worm, Wallace?'

'I'm thinking it was that fucking worm, Wallace!' Bob snapped back. It was unlike Bob to be tetchy, but even more unlike him to swear. 'But what can we do?'

'Sort it all out and carry on,' Ward confirmed. The two went back to their tidying up while people walked past, hardly paying any attention to the work going on in the small booth.

'Good morning, gentlemen.' Bob and Ward both recognised the voice, silky smooth and full of smarm. They turned, Ward speaking first.

'Mr Copchase, funny you should show up—we were just talking about you.'

Ward glanced at Bob, whose eyes had narrowed, his face red. Bob was small and wiry, but he was one of those people you simply wouldn't mess with when angry.

'Did that little shit of a son of yours do this?' he spat at Bradley, walking towards him.

Bradley, who had stopped at the edge of the walkway, pulled out a mobile phone and held it up in front of Bob's face. 'My ... *son* took this video about an hour ago as he was coming into the hall. Thought you'd be interested to see it.'

Bob stopped, suspiciously eyeing both Bradley and the phone held out in front of him. It was one of the new Nokia models that he had read about, with the screen that swivelled out—typical that the Copchases would already have these. But it was Ward who stepped forward, and Bradley let him take it, the smug look on his face remaining in anticipation of what they were about to watch. Bradley had obviously been looking forward to this, and would relish this moment.

Bob stood alongside Ward, watching the screen over his shoulder. The timer at the bottom of the screen told them the footage was taken at 9.48 am—roughly an hour ago. Occasionally someone would walk in front of the view, so whoever had filmed it must have been standing in the crowd of people flooding into the hall. They saw the Haywood's booth as they had left it the night before, but with a lone figure walking slowly around the booth from wall to wall, looking at the photos and reading the text. The figure then crouched to look at some more posters lower down on the wall, before suddenly standing up—at which point the video cut out.

'Who's that?' Ward asked.

Bob had known exactly who it was as soon as he saw the man's stance and stature in the video. 'That's Jamie,' he said quietly and turned to look at Ward.

'Yes, it is, isn't it?' came the smooth voice from behind them. 'Looks like you're accusing the wrong person again, Haywood. Best to get your facts straight first, eh?'

Ward glanced at Bob, who looked like he would explode if pushed any further. Around them, throngs of people were coming and going, oblivious to the altercation taking place in this small booth.

'Looks like your bad boy is back, Haywood, and this time he's got it in for *you*.'

Bob looked down to the floor; he had nothing more to say. Ward handed the phone back to Bradley.

'Get lost,' Ward said sternly but quietly. Bradley took his phone and walked away, laughing.

FaB-Ex '07

1

Ward was on his own this year. Bob had said he needed a break from FaB-Ex, that he was getting too old for it, but Ward knew the real reason: Bob couldn't bear to see Bradley Copchase any more. He could do his best to avoid the man, but he felt certain that Bradley would also do *his* best to make sure their paths crossed. Ward understood and knew Bob wouldn't be able to stay away for long. He'd be back next year.

The company had taken on a couple of new guys a few months ago, and Ward had set up all the stands with them the day before, finishing with their own booth, which only took a few minutes. They had gone home last night, leaving Ward on his own, and he was now looking forward to the few days ahead of him. He knew the company and its operations like the back of his hand and, although he was no salesman, he was always happy to talk about what Haywood's did to anyone who asked him.

Bob had called him late morning to ask how it was going, but Ward knew he really just wanted to know if he had seen anything of Bradley Copchase.

'... And no, I haven't seen him yet, Bob.'

Bob laughed. 'Am I that transparent? Give him my very best, won't you, when you see him.'

'I will, of course,' Ward had assured him and hung up. He knew the incident with Jamie last year laid heavily on Bob's mind. Bob had considered himself a father figure to Jamie and thought the world of him at one time. Why would Jamie have wrecked the stand?

'Ward!' A cheery voice called along the walkway, and Ward turned to see Don Caravello approaching, a big smile on his face and his hand outstretched ready to shake. Over the previous twelve months, thanks to Don's intervention, the company he worked for had become one of Haywood's biggest accounts. Gloucester Valves had also branched out to become Gloucester Process Solutions and were now involved in turnkey projects and complete fit-outs, using Haywood's for all their big jobs.

The two shook hands warmly and decided to go for lunch together. Ward glanced around the booth to make sure it was fit to leave and that there was nothing worth taking.

'I have something for you,' Don said as they walked towards the coffee shop.

'Another job?' Ward asked enthusiastically.

Don laughed. 'Not today—but soon,' he reassured. 'It's actually something for Bob, if you wouldn't mind passing it on to him, I think he'll be interested.'

Ward nodded, as Don fished about in his coat pocket and pulled out a CD. It was just the disc in a plastic case, and written in indelible pen on the disc in scruffy handwriting was 'Hall 3 Entry, FaB-Ex 2006, Day 1'.

'What's this?' Ward asked.

Don smiled. 'Bob told me about the incident with Jamie last year. Just so happens I know the organisers here. That's the footage from that camera there ...' He pointed to high up on the wall, directly above the main entrance to Hall 3. There was a CCTV camera on a bracket, pointing down into the hall and aimed directly at the Haywood's booth. 'It's from Day 1 last year; get Bob to watch it.'

'What's on it?'

'I'm not saying any more,' Don replied smugly, 'just ask Bob to watch it.'

They arrived at the coffee shop and skirted round the low bench that Wallace had fallen backwards over a few years before in such spectacular style.

'Mind the bench,' Don laughed.

Ward smiled, the memory coming back to him. 'I hope they've changed the carpets.'

FaB-Ex '08

1

Jamie knew what he had to do, and he had never been more nervous in his life.

His last twenty-four months had been a roller coaster. Within a few days of FaB-Ex the year before last, Baumgarten's had told him that he had failed to complete his probation period to their satisfaction and could no longer continue with them. He had returned his toolbox and overalls to the head office and finished that same day. He had no idea why; he had received nothing but glowing reports for all his installations and the work he had done for them. The only occasional negative was that a customer would say that he was quiet and didn't tend to interact much, but they often qualified this with a further comment to say they had no issue with this as his work was to such a high standard. He couldn't understand it.

Being made redundant was a setback to his recovery, but not as big as he would have imagined. He had done well; he had finished a couple of courses of the ECT shock therapy, and the specialist had told him that he could see a marked improvement. Jamie had also worked out a recipe for self-preservation: he knew what situations caused him angst and did his best to avoid them. If forced into them, he now had ways of coping—happy places he could retreat to and a persona that he could adopt temporarily to get him through.

He had made a massive effort in other areas of his life and now prioritised these over his work, which he saw as secondary. With the improved balance that he felt, he was confident he could get another job. He had found a few hobbies that he used as escapism, particularly photography and gardening. In fact, his love of gardening had led to a few jobs on the side, which had got him through financially after being terminated by Baumgarten's.

Josh was twelve now and doing really well at school. His results were good, and he was showing a mechanical aptitude that Jamie was very proud of. He was in the second cricket team and was getting batting coaching, which Jamie went along to when he could. Alison worked shifts now and she and David had a new baby, so Jamie would take Josh most weekends to help them out. Alison was a different person these days, and Jamie now got along well both with her and with David.

Then, quite out of the blue a week ago, he had received a text message from Bob Haywood, asking how he was and if he would be at the upcoming FaB-Ex. Not wanting to admit that he was out of work, Jamie had answered that he would be there, to which Bob had replied that it would be great to see him again and to please drop by the stand at the entrance to Hall 3, whenever he had the time.

It had seemed like a good idea at the time, but here he was now in the Piazza at the NEC, with the main entrance to Hall 3 in front of him. He sensed his peripheral vision starting to blur, a sure sign that he was nervous. The world appeared to be closing in around him, and his palms were sweating. He stood motionless as people swarmed to left and right, oblivious of the man standing motionless in their way.

Jamie needed his self-preservation recipe now, more than ever. He closed his eyes and turned his head to the floor, extending his fingers outwards on both hands as far as he could. He took a deep breath and held it, then pictured Josh helping him in the garden, his innocent smiling face full of love and happiness. The thought made him smile and he opened his eyes, raising his head and breathing out slowly. He was ready, and began walking forwards through the entry doors in a straight line, people around him having to divert their course. He paused as he went through for his visitor's badge to be scanned, smiled at the lady and carried on walking.

Ahead of him he could see the Haywood's booth. It was bigger than it had been two years before when he had run off, possibly double the size, with two high tables now and about eight or so high stools. There was also a counter, like a bar, towards the back of the booth, with all the brochures and business cards displayed.

This was a big step for Jamie; he had a lot of respect for the people he was about to see, but what did they think of him? He wasn't sure. Bob's messages had seemed friendly, so he had no reason to be concerned, and what did he have to lose, anyway? He had dressed up specially—no blue overalls today; he was in a shirt and tie, which he checked nervously as he approached the stand.

His timing was perfect. Bob was at one table and hung up his phone as Jamie watched, then made some notes on a piece of paper. Bob looked exactly the same as when Jamie had last seen him, possibly slightly less hair.

At the other table, Ward shook a visitor's hand and they parted ways, the visitor walking off along the walkway as Ward sat back down on a stool. He had put on a bit of weight but otherwise looked the same, too. Behind Ward's wider frame Jamie could see another man seated at the rear of the stand, but his back was turned and Jamie couldn't make him out.

Jamie didn't pause; he could do this. He walked straight onto the booth, and in his best mock-confident voice said, 'Hi, Bob ... Ward ... how are you?'

2

Bob looked up from his notepad, and his face broke into the widest smile. 'Jamie!'

He stepped out from round the high table, knocking a pen off as he did so, and held his arms out. Jamie raised an arm to shake his hand, but Bob ignored it and hugged him instead, slapping the younger man on the shoulder. 'My boy, it's wonderful to see you, how are you?'

Jamie hugged him back; it was the most natural thing in the world. After what seemed like an age, Bob let him go and shook his hand. Jamie turned to his side to see Ward also offering his hand. Jamie took it and shook it warmly. Neither man spoke, but both smiled and nodded; there was an understanding between them, no words were needed.

Bob still had his arm around Jamie's shoulder and pulled him to one side so that he could now see the third man on the stand, who had turned round and got to his feet. Jamie couldn't believe it—his emotions must be getting the better of him. There was the smile he knew so well, although its owner was much thinner and more frail than he remembered, and also with possibly less hair. It was Chilly.

'What the ...?' Jamie was lost for words.

Bob and Ward parted, allowing Chilly to come forward. He held both arms out and gave Jamie another hug.

'Come here, you useless git,' he said.

It was too much for Jamie. He felt the tears running down his cheeks onto Chilly's shoulders, and he did his best not to start shaking as he knew Chilly would simply take the mickey.

'Come on then, let go, ya pansy,' Chilly said, trying to free himself from Jamie's grip. 'You'll set my pacemaker off, and I can't go through all that shit again.'

'But ... I thought you had called it a day?' Jamie stammered.

'What, and miss all this fun? Naaah, mate. I did take a year off, though, after my surgery and such, but Gayle couldn't stand me kicking round the house all day.'

Jamie couldn't believe it. He knew that Chilly had survived the heart attack—but only just—and had wondered if he would ever see his old friend again.

As the two parted, Bob could see that Jamie was in no state to talk and offered an explanation.

'Retirement wasn't suiting him,' he smiled, nodding towards Chilly, who hadn't taken his eyes off Jamie. Jamie wiped his wet cheeks in embarrassment. 'So I've taken him back on as a consultant and site supervisor. No tools, no lifting; I'm under strict orders from Mrs Winterbottom—who, incidentally, tells me he is actually less stressed and easier to live with at home since he came back to work.'

Jamie laughed and glanced again at Chilly, but turned away again quickly when he realised it would set him off once more.

In an instinctive reaction for all four of them, each put their arms around the next, forming a ring, their heads almost touching. People walking past must have wondered if it was some kind of strange sales ritual. Bob turned to Jamie, next to him in the ring.

'Fancy your job back?'

Jamie still couldn't speak and had started to sniff. He nodded vigorously without thinking, like a child being offered the best toy in the world.

Bob turned to the other two. 'You guys okay with that?'
Both nodded and smiled at Jamie.
'Well, then, the old gang looks like it's back together.'

3

Jamie had his best week in years. He felt so comfortable in the company of Bob, Chilly and Ward, and they had a lot to catch up on. Bob spent most of Day 1 in meetings but had assured Jamie that he would spend all of Day 3 with him. Chilly and Ward had brought him up to speed on what he had missed since he had left, and he had enjoyed simply wandering round the show with Chilly, spending time with his old friend. He told Jamie how he had been close to death, and of the terrible pain in his chest. His cardiologist had since confided that it was the quick reactions of those around him at the time that had saved his life.

'Who would have ever guessed I'd owe you my life?'

Jamie put his arm around him. 'Just please don't do it again.' They were in Hall 4, walking for the sake of it, not really paying any attention to the stands on either side of them.

'What about you, mate? How are you doing?' Chilly asked. 'I hear you've not had it easy?'

Jamie didn't like to talk about his problems, except to his specialist; somehow, to talk to another bloke about it was almost like admitting weakness. With Chilly, though, it was different, and Jamie found himself opening up to him, being honest about the stupid things he had done and of the depths he had sunk to at his worst—even admitting that he had contemplated suicide after his mother had died.

'I never want to go back there again, Chill',' he admitted.

Chilly changed the subject and asked about Josh. It was a gamble, but it paid off, and Jamie's whole outlook seemed to change as he gushed about his boy, how good he was at maths and the quick-fire twenty he had hit in the seconds' match on Saturday. Chilly made a mental note that this was the motherlode. Jamie told Chilly about Alison, how they communicated far better since they were divorced than they ever did when they were married and how he and her new husband, David, got on famously.

They were in the Piazza now, crossing to the entrance to Hall 3 and back to the Haywood's booth. Chilly asked Jamie about his work and how he had survived since losing his job with Baumgarten's almost two years earlier.

'Well, I did gardening jobs around the area for a while and then managed to get part-time work mowing lawns and helping out at the old folks' home—you know, the one Mum was in. I still had a lot of spare time though, so I finally finished renovating the family home.'

Chilly nodded. He remembered offering Jamie help with it and was relieved that that old offer was now off the table.

'Re-did the main bathroom,' Jamie continued, 'new plumbing, central heating, nice fitted kitchen, created ensuites for each of the bedrooms, new roof, and of course, made the best I could with the garden—fully landscaped.'

'Blimey!' Chilly was impressed.

'Yes.' Jamie's voice dropped to a whisper. 'Then I sold it for an absolute mint, almost triple what I was hoping for. There were two or three families interested, all trying to outbid one another, it was incredible—so please don't say anything, but I'm actually quite comfortably off.'

Chilly made the schoolboy pretence of zipping his lips and smiled. 'I know who to come to for a loan then,' he said. 'So where are you living?'

'Oh, same old flat I had when I was first married; suits me perfectly as a single man. Also I was told by the specialist that as part of my recovery, I shouldn't change my surroundings, should keep everything as it was. Apparently moving house is a big unsettler, like a divorce or being fired.'

They were back on the booth now, and both Bob and Ward were talking to people separately at the two tables.

Jamie frowned. 'Anyway, how did you know about Baumgarten's letting me go?'

'I guess you probably don't know why they fired you?' Chilly asked, his voice quiet.

'No, never worked it out,' Jamie admitted. 'Just assumed they felt I was a liability or something. I was advised not to contest it, was told it was their prerogative and that I didn't have a leg to stand on—so I just put it behind me and moved on.'

Bob, now free, moved across to join them. He opened his mouth to speak, but Chilly got in first.

'I think you should show him, Bob.'

Bob nodded and beckoned Jamie across to the bar at the rear of the stand, where his laptop was open. Without saying anything, Bob moved his finger round the mouse pad, occasionally clicking, then finally spinning the laptop for Jamie to see the screen.

'You lost your job at Baumgarten's because you were wrongly blamed for this.'

On the screen was a still photograph of the smaller Haywood's booth in Hall 3 from a few years earlier; Jamie recognised it from when he had popped in to look at the photos around the walls. But it had been trashed. The table and chairs were lying on the floor, the posters and photos had been torn off the walls or slashed, and the booth was littered with business cards and brochures. It was a mess.

'What?' Jamie's mind did somersaults. 'But I didn't do that ... and who ... How did Baumgarten's find out?'

Bob dropped his head to look at Jamie, as if looking over the rim of glasses he wasn't wearing. 'Someone sent them this photograph and said that they had seen you do it. Baumgarten's of course asked for proof, and a video was sent to them that showed you standing in the booth a few minutes earlier, studying the pictures and clearly looking upset.'

'But I didn't—why would I—?'

Bob put his hand on Jamie's arm. 'I know, I know, don't upset yourself. Unfortunately, the circumstantial evidence was too much for Baumgarten's to take the risk, and you were still on probation, so the easiest thing to do was make something up and just get rid of you.'

'But why? I don't get it, who would—?' Jamie stopped in mid sentence, and Bob held up a finger to pause him.

'Now, do you remember our old friend Don? Don Caravello? Used to be at Steelfab, then he moved to Gloucester Process Solutions?' Bob asked.

Jamie nodded. In his mind, Don was the man who had married his lovely Penny. He sighed, the reminder of the past coming up from the depths for a split second. Bob spun the laptop round and pressed 'play' on a video.

'Well, Don knows the FaB-Ex organisers and managed to get hold of the CCTV video from that morning.' He pointed up at the camera on the wall above the entrance, aimed right at them. 'Now just watch.'

The picture wasn't great, but Jamie could make out the main entrance to Hall 3, with people flooding in and the Haywood's booth right in the centre of the screen. It was all set up, but there was no one on it. Every now and then someone would step out of the crush of people onto the booth carpet as a shortcut to get round someone else, but otherwise all the people were on the main thoroughfares.

Then, as he watched, someone stepped out of the crowd and into the booth. It was as if the single person was in slow motion, and all the hordes of people around him had been sped up. Jamie knew it was him; he remembered that morning so well, those few minutes. He had wanted a glimpse into his past to remind himself of happy times, but all it did was hurt him. He took a deep breath and carried on watching.

In the video the man put his toolbox down and looked one by one at each of the posters, crouching down at one point to read some low text. Bob pointed to a still figure in the throng of people passing the stand.

'Notice him? He's the guy taking the video of you that was sent to Baumgarten's.'

Jamie watched himself stand up quickly, pick up his toolbox and almost run off the stand.

'That's you gone,' Bob commented. 'Now watch our friend in the crowd here.'

The man who had been standing still in the swarming crowd now stepped into the booth and, without looking back or around him, started to spread the business cards and brochures on the floor to make it look like someone had thrown them. He was extremely calm and didn't attract attention by looking up or acting suspiciously. He then laid the table and chairs down on the carpet and started to tear the posters off the walls and rip them up. The whole process took under a minute before he walked off the booth carpet, turned and took a photo of the damage with his mobile phone, then disappeared back into the moving crowd.

Jamie was speechless and turned to look at Bob, who said it for him. 'You were framed, son.'

Jamie's mouth was hanging open and, aware that he must have looked quite gormless, he closed it.

'Guess who sent the photo and video to Baumgarten's?' Bob asked. Jamie shook his head, although he knew who and he knew why. 'It was Bradley Copchase, but he claimed it was Wallace who saw you do it. He told Baumgarten's that Wallace was so shocked at what you were doing, that he actually stopped videoing.'

Jamie nodded; Wallace had been easy to identify in the video. 'Okay, so we're even,' he said. 'I deserved that. I humiliated him, and I hurt him.'

Chilly had overheard Jamie's last remark. 'Bollocks did you deserve that,' he said. 'That runt was asking for everything you did to him.'

Bob held up a hand to stop him going any further.

'So now you know,' he said to Jamie. 'Have a think and let me know what you want me to do. The choice is yours, but whatever you decide I'll back you one hundred percent.'

4

Day 3 of the show was coming quickly. Bob had managed to find a late cancellation in the hotel and booked Jamie in. Jamie, meanwhile, had driven home late on Day 1 to pick up a washkit and some fresh clothes so that they were able to stay together as a group. There was still plenty to talk about.

On the evening of Day 2, the four of them had all had a meal together in a curry house in the city, then caught a taxi back to the NEC. Bob and Chilly were tired and excused themselves to retire to bed. Ward had to phone home, as there was some issue with one of his boys at school and he needed to speak to his wife, Diane. This left Jamie on his own, and he was tempted to go back to his room as well.

But he felt good. After years in a pit of despair, taking one blow after another, he was beginning to feel like his fortunes were changing. He never imagined he would be back working with Haywood's, and yet here he was. His home life was good—not great, but good. Josh was doing well, and Jamie had money in the bank. His condition, as he had been told to call it, was under control, and he had not only learned to live with it but was doing well in spite of it. He had no one to share his life with, but he didn't have much luck in that department and, as an only child, he had learned to get by perfectly well on his own. And now he knew and understood why he had been sacked, something he thought he would not get to the bottom of, and had consciously pushed to the back of his mind. So what was he going to do about it?

He sat down at the bar in the hotel and ordered a pint of lager. The last time he had sat here was when Chilly had had his heart attack. That didn't matter any more, because Chilly was fine now; it no longer needed to be a painful memory, as it had been wiped out by the present. The pint was put in front of him, and he charged it to his room. There was another occasion he had spent time at this bar, many years earlier, when he had been Billy-no-mates and had met Bad Penny. He smiled. That was a good memory and always had been; it represented a carefree time when he had no ties or responsibilities—happy days indeed.

He mulled over his current situation and compared it to where he had come from in the last few years. Did he really now want to get involved in an act of retaliation on Wallace and Bradley Copchase? What would it mean—court battles? Possibly not. But it would certainly mean facing the Copchases again, something he wasn't keen to do. And what would it bring him if he won? A short-term sense of exacted revenge? An ongoing enemy he didn't need? It would certainly mean a painful few months, and even if all Wallace did was ask for an apology, it would be disruptive and unnecessary at a time when Jamie felt he was repairing well.

He took a big sip of his beer. Decision made: he would not take any action. He would get on with his life and leave things exactly as they were.

FaB-Ex '09

1

A year later to the day, Jamie found himself back in the exact same location, sitting at the bar in the hotel, on his own with a pint of lager. Again, Bob and Ward had retired early, but Jamie didn't mind; he enjoyed his own company.

It was just Bob, Ward and Jamie at FaB-Ex this year. Chilly was away on holiday, in a caravan on the Isle of Wight. They missed him, but he would be back at work in a couple of weeks. He was down to three days a week now anyway, on the rundown to his second retirement, which he was teased about no end.

Jamie looked around him from his seat at the bar. He was comfortable here; it was like a home he had lived in for decades. There were both good and bad memories associated with his time at FaB-Ex, but overall it was a comfortable place for him to be. It was almost like a sanctuary—he felt safe here.

But Bob had dropped a bombshell on them today, something that could upset the status quo and change things permanently. It was now possible Jamie may not be back here next year: Bob was selling the business. He hadn't formally started the process yet or had the business valued, but he was scouting around to see if it was a feasible proposition. Jamie sighed heavily and took a big sip of his beer.

A group of women sitting at a nearby table erupted into laughter, breaking him out of his train of thought. He looked across at them, and the two women facing him noticed him look, realised they were being loud, and shushed the other two. Jamie smiled and turned away; the last thing he wanted to do was attract attention. It reminded him of the evening he had first met Penny. There had been four girls, then two, and then one, who had stayed with him in the bar after Chilly had gone to bed. The memory made him smile and he went with it, recalling the two of them laughing openly, two complete strangers—a beautiful salesgirl and a rough apprentice. They would have looked so mismatched. Or would they? Did it matter? They had hit it off immediately and then got on so well, in every sense.

Jamie felt himself growing melancholy and tried to change his thoughts. His condition was well and truly under control now, and in fact he had formally been discharged from the care of his specialist. After six very difficult years, he was out of the medical system; he had been told he shouldn't need the shock therapy any more, and the specialist had said that he hoped never to have to see him again. He felt good, he felt under control, he enjoyed his life. The turning point had actually come just before he had rejoined Haywood's last year, but there was no doubt that getting his old job back and returning to the familiar had been a major contributor to his current stability.

'Mind if I join you?'

The gentle voice snapped him out of his stupor, and he looked along the bar to see a woman climbing up onto the next stool. He did mind, but he didn't want to be rude; it wasn't in his nature. He had been enjoying his own company and hoping for a bit of time to come to terms with the fact that Bob was selling the business.

'No, of course. Can I get you a drink?' he heard himself ask. He recognised her as one of the four women who had been laughing so loudly. Their table was empty now, and there was no sign of any of the other three women.

'Thank you, I'll have a Prosecco,' she answered with a smile.

She was average height with tinted fair hair, and probably in her late thirties. She wore glasses and was dressed in a dark blue two-piece suit and white blouse. Jamie wondered what he must look like; he hadn't looked in a mirror for about twelve hours and probably needed a shave and some fresh deodorant. Still, it didn't matter; he would have a polite drink and then find a reason to excuse himself.

The Prosecco arrived and Jamie slid it along the bar towards her. 'I'm Jamie,' he said.

'Hi, Jamie, I'm Cassie. Nice to meet you,' and she tipped the glass at him.

2

The more she drank, the more she talked, but Jamie didn't mind that. He wasn't much of a conversationalist, and if she hadn't led the conversation it would almost certainly have died and there would have been awkward silences. He simply sat and listened and nodded occasionally. He had mastered the art of looking interested, and as long as she didn't throw it back at him and ask him a question, he was quite content to listen and simply be carried along on the wave.

They were on their second drinks now; she had ordered another round without even asking Jamie, and the pint of lager had duly appeared. She seemed nice, clearly well presented and well educated, but more than that, she had a gentle character. When she turned away, Jamie took the opportunity to look her up and down. In another lifetime, she would have been his kind of person, whatever that meant—the sort of woman he would have been attracted to.

At the moment, though, he needed routine in his life; he needed normality without change, and a partner or a girlfriend meant change. He felt sure the time would come when he would feel ready, but not yet. His first and most immediate obstacle was to get his head around the fact that Bob was going to sell the business. At best he would have someone new to report to, despite Bob's assurances that he would want to be kept on in a consultative capacity for at least a couple of years to ease himself into retirement. At worst, he would lose his job, and he would be back where he was twelve months ago. Or would he? He had been back in the workforce for a full year now and was guaranteed a good reference from Bob.

He wasn't proud of himself, as he still found himself nodding at Cassie's ongoing banter but had absolutely no idea what she was talking about. He wasn't sure if he had missed a nod or nodded in the wrong place, but she stopped talking and cocked her head to one side.

'What about you?' she asked, quite out of the blue. 'What's going on in Jamie's life?'

He had been put on the spot, and Jamie felt his palms grow clammy. Public speaking had always been one of his worst phobias, but his recent issues had accentuated it to the point where he became nervous even in a one-on-one situation, particularly with someone he didn't know well. She saw the look on his face and put a hand on his knee briefly.

'Sorry,' she said, 'I didn't mean to pry.'

Jamie felt bad that the conversation had been one-sided and that he hadn't given her any attention. He pulled himself together and answered.

'No, it's fine,' he said, and then, thinking that he had nothing to lose and needed something to talk about that wouldn't make him look weird, 'I found out today that the company I work for is going to be sold. Well, it's going up for sale, so I'm not sure if I'll be out of a job soon.'

Cassie nodded. 'I'm sorry to hear that.' She looked quite genuine, like she was actually concerned for this quiet stranger. 'I wouldn't worry about it too much, though. I think when businesses are sold, as long as they're not broken up, the new owners tend to keep the current employees on. Why would they replace them? They're the ones who keep the company going and will keep it going during the transition period.' She sounded like she knew what she was talking about. 'The only people who should be nervous are the managers—you know, the dead wood that costs the company money. I think trimming is often done at a higher level. Are you a manager?'

Jamie laughed. The question surprised him, but he reminded himself that he was sitting there in a shirt and tie, rather than his more usual overalls. 'No, I'm not. I supervise work on-site, and apart from a brief gap, I've been with the company for years now.'

'You should be fine then; I wouldn't worry about it.' Jamie found her words reassuring and nodded. 'One of the companies I used to work for went up for sale,' she continued, 'and in the end there was some kind of management buy-out.'

'How does that work?' Jamie asked. 'I've heard of them but don't know what it means.'

'I'm not too sure either,' Cassie answered after a sip of her wine. 'Basically, a group of the managers pooled their money and bought the business, then just kept it running as it was. They kept all the employees, and apart from a new company name, we didn't really notice any difference.'

For once, Jamie was paying attention. 'That's interesting,' he said. He picked up his beer and swigged back the last mouthful. 'Tell me more,' he smiled at her, 'even if only to reassure me that I won't lose my job.'

Jamie ordered another round of drinks and charged them to his room. Cassie tried to remember as much as she could about the management takeover, but by her own admittance it had been a few years ago and at the time she, like Jamie now, only really cared that she would keep her job. Jamie watched her knock back her third glass very quickly; her drinking seemed to be speeding up, and he wondered if this also was affecting her ability to stay on one subject. Jamie heard about all her co-workers, the open-plan offices and each of the managers in turn who bought the business. He didn't mind; it had given him an idea and was happy to listen.

Cassie picked up her wine glass only to find it empty, and seemed surprised. 'Another?' she asked.

Jamie had barely touched his third. 'I'm fine,' he said, 'but please, you go ahead.'

She nodded at the barman and pointed at her empty glass, before looking back at Jamie. 'You married?' she asked.

The question caught Jamie by surprise, and he felt his mouth open and his eyebrows raise inadvertently. It took a second for him to get his head around the question, and he felt her eyes boring into him.

'No,' he answered honestly, 'I was, but not any more.' He wasn't sure why, but he held up his left ring finger as if in proof. There was no ring on it, and no white line to indicate it had been recently removed.

She nodded and smiled. 'Girlfriend?'

'No.'

'Turned gay?' Jamie was shocked by this one, but Cassie started laughing. 'Just kidding!' she added.

'No,' he confirmed again, but then didn't know what else to add. She was clearly now quite drunk, and Jamie could tell by this recent line of questioning that she was trying to make a move. He liked her, she seemed a nice enough person, but he just wasn't ready for this.

'I'm sorry,' he said as gently as he could, 'I'd really prefer to leave it here.'

She smiled and nodded at him, then touched him gently on the knee once more. 'Why is it the good ones are either married, gay or just too bloody decent?' She took her hand away, and Jamie was relieved to see that she didn't seem too upset. 'I'll leave you with your thoughts.' She collected her bag from the bar, and swung it over her shoulder. 'Hopefully

I'll see you tomorrow?' she offered as she looked over her shoulder. Jamie nodded and smiled back without speaking, then turned back to face the bar as she walked out.

He knew he'd done the right thing. A relationship at any level was still probably outside his capabilities at this moment. One thing at a time.

FaB-Ex '10

1

It was going to be a hot day. One of those rare British true-summer days, when the morning is full of promise and you can tell by about 9 am that it's going to be a scorcher. The air conditioning was already on in Hall 3 in anticipation, so the huge hall was actually a bit cold when she walked into it at 9.45 am.

The first thing she saw was the Haywood's booth directly in front of her and at least one familiar face. She changed direction and went across to say hello.

Bob Haywood was putting out brochures as she walked up, and he didn't see her until she was right next to him.

'Good morning, stranger,' she offered. Bob almost jumped, as though he had been in his own little world.

It took him half a second to place her. 'Oh, hi!' He held out his hand. 'You used to do our brochures, a few years back.'

'That's right.'

'In fact, we still use the photo of you.' He pointed to the photo of the two of them shaking hands, low down on one wall as part of one of the larger Haywood's posters. 'So what are you up to now, still with the same crowd?'

'I changed jobs a couple of years ago,' she answered. 'I'm an accounts manager with the Ditto Group. We sell pipework and fittings to transport liquids, beverages and such. Don't get me started, I'll end up giving you my sales pitch.'

'And that's why you're back here?'

'Yes, back again at FaB-Ex,' she replied, 'back like a bad penny, as my dear old grandma would have said.' Bob smiled; he had heard the phrase before. 'So what's happening at Haywood's? You must be doing okay if your stand is front and centre in Hall 3.'

'Every year now,' Bob confirmed. 'It's become sort of our allotted spot; the management approach us first about this booth, because they know it's an easy one to fill. Plus we like the location—the first stand visitors see as they walk in, and it's good for security.' He gestured to the CCTV camera above the main entry doors that was pointing directly at them. 'But yes, work's really good. I'm stepping down soon as MD and owner, though —I'm selling the business.'

'Oh, That's fantastic—well, fantastic for you at least. Are you planning to retire?'

'Semi-retiring,' Bob confirmed, 'I'm going to stay on a few days a week, in a consultative capacity, you understand.' He winked at her slyly. 'My wife won't want me round the house seven days a week, and this company has been my life for so long that I'm not sure what I'd do if one Monday morning I just wasn't involved any more.'

'So have you found a buyer?'

Bob nodded enthusiastically. 'Yes, one of my guys is buying it, so I'm delighted—it's almost like passing it on to a son. He sold the family home a few years back, so he can buy most of it as a lump sum, and the rest he'll pay off with a loan. I was keen for him to take it, so I've done him a good deal.'

'Wow, that's a result! It must have made the process easy?'

'It did, yes. Hasn't all gone through yet, but should be finalised in about six months. He decided to buy into in a business that he knows rather than another property, and it gives him job security as well as an investment. You'd probably know him—Jamie—he's been with us forever.'

She thought, pursing her lips and looking skyward. 'No, I don't think so. I knew an apprentice once from your company, I think his name was Craig.'

'Craig?' Bob frowned. 'Oh Jesus, that guy? He left years ago. He wasn't our greatest success.'

She nodded, and a strange feeling passed over her. She didn't like hearing he wasn't a great success; her memory of him was that he had been thorough and diligent. But what did she know?

Chilly walked up. 'Hello, I recognise you,' he said, offering a hand and a warm smile. 'Correct me if I'm wrong, but weren't you a Wow! girl?'

She looked Chilly up and down. She too recognised him, though he was fifteen years older and had lost a lot of weight.

'Yes, I was! There were four of us. I remember you, too—don't tell me ... Billy, Willy ...?'

'Chilly,' Chilly confirmed, 'everyone calls me Chilly.' She shook his hand. She remembered now—she had asked if he was called Chilly because his backside was always out in the open air and had been told it wasn't, but she couldn't now recall the real reason or the story behind the name.

'I'd like to say I remember your face,' Chilly said cheekily, 'but in those days it wasn't your faces that we noticed.' He roared with laughter at his own comment, which made the other two laugh. Coming from anyone else, it would have been a sexist remark, but Chilly, in his inimitable way, seemed to be able to get away with it.

She noticed Bob quickly change the subject before Chilly dragged it down a path it couldn't reverse out of. 'So if you sell pipework, you must need fit-outs and installations?' he asked.

'Now who's giving the sales pitch?' She laughed, then added, more seriously, 'yes, we absolutely do. I'm only here for a few hours—one of my accounts is here this morning at the show, and then I've got to go, but I'm sure our operations guys would be interested in getting a better idea of what you do.'

'They should meet Jamie,' Bob said. 'He's the future of the business, not us two dinosaurs, but he's gone off to buy the sandwiches for lunch and some more waters for the stand.'

'Great! I'll send someone across to see him later, say hello and chat to him,' she said and started to make her way off the stand with a wave.

'Lovely, thanks for dropping by.' Both Bob and Chilly gave a half-wave as she left, but carried on watching her as she walked away off the stand and onto the walkway.

'Ah, if I were only twenty years younger,' Chilly commented with a sigh.

Bob put his hand on his colleague's shoulder. 'What, and give yourself another heart attack?'

The two were interrupted as Jamie walked onto the stand from the opposite direction, carrying a cardboard box. He paused briefly and sniffed the air, as if he had caught a familiar smell. He narrowed his eyes as if recalling a distant memory and looked to his left and right, but the moment was gone.

'Right, guys,' he said, 'I've got sandwiches, water ... and most importantly, coffees.'

2

Alison had called Jamie the week before and asked him to explain to Josh exactly what he did for a living. Apparently, Josh had asked, and the best Alison could come up with was, 'I know he assembles things and I know he carries a toolbox around a lot.' Jamie had laughed at this description. It might have been reasonably accurate in the past, particularly when he and Alison were together, but even then it was a very simplified overview.

He and Alison had actually shared a rare laugh together over the phone. 'Why does he want to know?' he had asked.

'He's starting to think about which college course to do when he finishes, and then what type of job he wants to move on to once he's qualified,' Alison had answered. 'I think they all had a brief chat with the careers adviser today, so it's set him thinking, and he's been asking a lot of questions.'

It also set Jamie thinking. Josh was a bright young man and clearly had a mechanical aptitude, which he was keen to exploit. Alison had asked him if he would be able to spend time with Josh on his next visit, explaining what his options were and describing what Jamie had done for a living in the years since finishing school. Jamie had had a better idea: with FaB-Ex coming up, he arranged to spend a half-day there with his son, showing him around and giving him an insight into the world of engineering, process and commerce.

It had to be the Saturday morning, the last day of the show, as Josh was tied up on weekdays. That didn't matter to Jamie, and he had cleared it with his colleagues who would handle the stand in his absence.

On the day, FaB-Ex was abuzz. Visitors jostled to get through the doors into the halls, the main walkways were packed, and there was a feeling of energy under the huge overall roof. Jamie could not have picked a better day to demonstrate how the industry was thriving, though progress was slow through the crowds. Josh was feeding off the excitement that seemed to be all around him and was keen to see at first hand much of the equipment he had been taught about in theory at college.

'So is this valve automatic?' Josh asked. He had stopped to inspect a large piece of process equipment close to the edge of the walkway. Jamie smiled. It must be a good question because he actually didn't know the answer.

'Yes, it is,' he bluffed, only sixty percent sure. They were on the Pressto stand, which had been assembled by the two young apprentices under Ward's guidance and final approval. It did look really good, very professional and nicely laid out. If Jamie had been interested in buying this kind of equipment, there was no doubt he would have walked onto the stand for a closer look.

He had introduced Josh to the stand staff and asked if it was okay to show him the equipment. Josh had held out his hand to shake with each of the personnel, and Jamie was delighted to see the company's managing director ask him a few questions about his future and which direction he saw himself heading in. Josh had answered him fully and looked him in the eye, but hadn't come across as either cocky or nervous. Jamie had to forcefully remove the look of pride from his face.

Once the MD had wished them well, father and son had then spent some time looking over the equipment. Jamie found himself pulling out a tissue from his pocket a couple of times to remove grubby fingerprints from the stainless steel; old habits die hard.

'I did my own apprenticeship with Haywood's,' Jamie explained, 'so I've been putting the Pressto stands together for nearly twenty years now.'

'Oh wow!' It was genuine admiration. 'I'd love to do that,' Josh enthused. 'Do Haywood's still do apprenticeships?'

'They do,' Jamie confirmed, 'but they are hotly contested. If you want to get onto the shortlist, I'm afraid you'll have to do it based on your own merits—not because I'm your dad.'

'Of course,' Josh answered quickly. Jamie was relieved that this didn't seem to have come as a surprise to him.

'You'd be interviewed by Ward and Chilly, and they'd treat you exactly the same as all the other applicants.'

Josh didn't look up from the equipment. He was still hovering over the actuator for the valve at the base of a large piece of process equipment and ran his fingers along the pneumatic lines to trace their source.

'I wouldn't expect anything else,' he said. 'I don't want to get into a course that I'm not suited for.' Jamie nodded; once more he was impressed.

At that moment, a small group of girls walked past the end of the stand. Jamie noticed them pause their conversation as a couple noticed Josh. He was a well-presented young man with features somewhere between chiselled and rugged. Josh, tracing the pneumatic signal lines back to the main control panel, didn't even notice them. In that moment, Jamie realised that his fourteen year-old son was a far more rounded and balanced human being than he had ever been. He thought back to his first day at FaB-Ex and how Chilly had chastised him for being so easily distracted by the pretty girls from the Wow! stand.

After talking to another of the Pressto's team about the control panel, Josh and Jamie moved off the stand and headed along the main walkway past more equipment stands. Josh seemed genuinely interested in everything he saw and would pause occasionally for a closer look.

'Do you want me to speak to the guys about you applying for an apprenticeship, then?' Jamie asked.

'No need,' Josh replied dismissively, 'I'll ask Mr Haywood and Mr Winterbottom when we get back to the stand.' Jamie raised his eyebrows.

He really couldn't ask for any more. He pictured Wallace Copchase, a young man forced into a job he was unsuited for and who attracted criticism and derision from those who met him. Chilly called him Mini-Me, but the truth was that he was nothing like his father, Bradley. Wallace lacked the charm and charisma of Bradley and had minimal people skills; he would have been better in a role where interaction with colleagues was kept to a minimum and interaction with customers was eliminated completely. Jamie did not want this scenario repeated for his own son, and he was determined to avoid what he knew would be viewed as nepotism.

He looked at Josh as the young man laughed and joked with a man on a stand whose company looked like they manufactured packaging equipment for biscuits and cookies. Surely, the fact that Jamie was overtly aware of this possibility and was doing everything in his power to avoid Josh joining for the wrong reasons was more than enough to prove he was acting correctly. Josh and the man continued laughing together at some mutual joke, causing Jamie to smile. Josh and Wallace were very different people; Josh clearly had interpersonal skills, and his insistence that he wanted to approach Bob, Chilly and Ward himself spoke volumes.

Jamie heard Chilly's voice in his mind. 'Your boy wasn't born with a silver spoon in his mouth, mate—hasn't had smoke blown up his arse all his life like that worm Wallace. Don't you worry; as long as I have anything to do with the apprenticeships, he'll be hired on ability and trained exactly the same as all the other young nerks—just like you were.'

FaB-Ex '11

1

'Well, here's to your new managing director,' Bob toasted, wine glass raised. 'To Jamie!'

'To Jamie!'

Everyone around the table raised their glasses in Jamie's direction. He usually wasn't comfortable being the centre of attention, as it made him anxious, but in the present company he was all right with it. He knew all of these guys so well that they had become his support mechanism, and as a result he was almost back to 'normal'. Running the business had boosted his confidence; it was something he knew and understood well. He could talk about it to anyone, at length and with conviction. Buying Haywood's had been a good decision, both for his present well-being and for his future.

Each person had taken a sip and put their glasses down on the table, their faces now turned back to each other. All were drinking wine except Chilly, who was on bitter lemon, and the apprentices, who were on Coke. Bob had asked Chilly, 'Who drinks bitter lemon these days?' Chilly said he liked it because it reminded him of his childhood, when the R White's drinks van would toot its horn at the end of the driveway.

Jamie smiled as he looked at his old friend, who went on to discuss job titles under the new regime with Bob.

'I think I should be Bullshit Manager,' Chilly was saying.

'What, because you're full of it?' Bob laughed.

'No, dopey, because I'm the only person in this company that *doesn't* generate any, and you need me to manage all the crap the rest of you create. Maybe I could be the Haywood's official *Bullshit Containment Manager?'*

Jamie smiled as he listened, musing how when a group of men got together, they really could talk utter nonsense. He was proud of this team and proud to be leading them. He surprised himself in that he wasn't daunted at all.

Down at the far end of the table were two apprentices, whom he had taken on as an agreement with the local technical college. He and Chilly had interviewed about twenty candidates for the positions from all the students available and picked these two. He watched as they both laughed at Chilly's comments, finding him funny but not wanting to join in, as that would then inevitably make them the next target of the older man's coarse wit. They had learned quickly that it was best to keep quiet.

He had spoken to Bob and Chilly about Josh potentially joining the team at Haywood's as an apprentice and tried to picture him sitting at the end of the table where the two young men were now. He would be so proud if that happened; but with him now being the MD, he didn't want to be responsible for doing the same as Bradley Copchase, pushing his own son into a position that didn't suit him.

Bob and Chilly had agreed that they would interview Josh when the time came and would give an honest appraisal on his suitability. Josh was fifteen now; he would sit his final exams next summer and then planned to go to the same college these two apprentices attended. If all went well, he would start there in just over a year, and if he took the 'sandwich-course' option which mixed theory and practice, he could start with Haywood's soon after. Jamie couldn't be prouder.

Aware that the two apprentices were a bit out of the group by being at the far end of the table, he called out, 'Will, Dinesh, come up this end—swap places with Bob and Chilly. Let these two old duffers argue on their own down the end there.'

Bob looked slightly affronted but Chilly just laughed, and the two older men, seeing the sense of the seat change, happily moved to the end of the table so that Jamie could talk to the two youngsters. 'We know our place,' Bob commented with a smile.

They were nice, well-rounded lads with a good attitude; still a bit green, but he knew Ward and Chilly would knock the sharp corners off them. Ward asked both of them about their hobbies, and Jamie was happy to sit and watch, listen to them discussing the latest models of Nikon camera and the relative benefits and prices of each.

Today had been Day 1 of the expo and the first time Jamie had been in charge at a FaB-Ex. He had enjoyed every second of it. The Haywood's team and their customers all seemed to have accepted him as the new head of the business. The only company he couldn't include in that, of course, was Steelfab, and he had decided that tomorrow, Day 2 of the show, would be the day he approached Bradley and Wallace and offered them an olive branch. He had nothing to lose by not doing it and nothing to gain by doing it, but his conscience told him it was the right thing to do. This sort of thing didn't seem to faze him any more, and for the first time in many years, Jamie felt really positive about the future.

Life really was good.

2

Don Caravello had been visiting the Haywood's stand now for at least an hour and had spent time with everyone, but mostly Bob and Ward. Jamie, meanwhile, was talking to Chilly and had mentioned to him that he was going to try and make his peace with the Steelfab guys.

'Are you insane? Why would you want to do that?' Chilly asked. 'Fuck 'em. They are lowlifes, pond scum ... wankers. Both of them.'

'Wankers? You guys talking about my old pals at Steelfab?' Don appeared next to them.

'Yes, we were, actually,' Jamie confirmed, laughing.

'Really? I was just joking.' Don slapped Jamie on the back. 'Just a stab in the dark. What have they done now?'

Jamie explained that as the new head of the business, he really should go and make his peace with the Copchases. It didn't help that every time their names were mentioned, Chilly would still call them 'Cockface' and Wallace either 'Mini-Me' or the 'Charisma Kid'.

'I'll come with you, if you want,' Don offered, 'just in case they say or do something. It's probably best to have a witness there with you, just in case.'

'Mini-me might piss himself again if he sees you, Don,' Chilly quipped.

Don turned to Chilly. 'Please don't take this the wrong way, but we might leave you behind, Chill'. I reckon this will require tact and diplomacy.'

Chilly laughed. 'Are you saying I can't be tactful? Well, you know where I am if you need me; just call and I'll be there.'

'Fancy going now?' Jamie asked.

'No time like the present,' Don replied, and the two men set off towards the exit.

'Give them my love!' Chilly called after them as they walked away, and they could still hear him shouting as they rounded the corner. 'I hope Mini-Me brought spare pants with him this year, he'll shit himself when he sees you two comin'!'

The two men looked at each other as they listened for more, but it appeared Chilly had finally run out of things to say.

'How are you these days, Jamie?'

Don's question was genuine, and Jamie had always liked him. He would have been told all about Jamie's problems, so there was no point holding back, but at the same time Jamie felt the most positive he had since his apprenticeship. He found himself opening up to Don, telling him about the battles he had had.

'I heard about Wallace's video,' Don said. 'If it had been me, I would have wanted to punch his lights out, so I thought you did well not to react to it.'

They paused, stopping at the side of the walkway to finish their conversation. They had both seen the Steelfab stand up ahead and wanted to finish their chat before facing the Copchases. There was no rush.

'How's your family?' Jamie asked, more to balance the conversation and show some interest.

'The girls are fine,' Don said, 'growing up too fast. Plenty of teenage angst, so there's never a dull moment—and the younger one isn't even a teenager yet. They certainly keep us on our toes, and don't start me on what they cost.'

'You've got two, haven't you?'

'Yes, Laura is eleven, and Emily is sixteen. Emily was Nat's from a previous relationship. She's interested in joining the Gloucester's sales training program, starting next year; she'd be great at it.'

Jamie was a sentence behind. 'Sixteen?' he asked. His blood had run cold.

'Yes. She's a lovely girl, bubbly, outgoing, the life and soul ... then there's Laura, she's a pain in the arse, and Nat reckons that's the influence of my DNA.'

Don laughed at his own comment, but Jamie's mind was a jumble. He couldn't get past the sixteen years of age. How long was it since he last saw Penny? He would have to work it out, but he reckoned the last time they had been together was seventeen years ago.

Jamie couldn't resist it. 'Do you know Emily's father? Is she still in touch with him?'

'No,' Don replied, 'no idea. Apparently it was some bloke Nat met at this show.'

It was getting worse. Jamie was starting to panic, and he needed to hide it. All he could think of to say was, 'And how's ... your wife?' He still struggled to say her name.

'She's not great, actually, Jamie; off work at the moment. We're not sure what's wrong. She's having blood tests and some scans later this week.'

Jamie frowned. He was pleased for the redirection of the conversation but didn't like the fact that Penny wasn't well. 'I'm sorry to hear that,' he said, and he meant it.

He needed to get away from Don. He needed to gather his thoughts, and more than anything he needed to sit quietly and work out dates.

'Actually, Don, I might not do this today.' He pointed towards the Steelfab stand. 'I've just remembered a few bits I need to do, if you don't mind?'

'Yes, of course,' Don replied, always accommodating. 'No problem, Jamie. I might go see them myself, anyway. They'll probably throw me off the stand, but who cares?'

They shook hands. 'You're a brave man, Don,' Jamie commented. 'Thanks for the chat. I'll see you later.'

They parted company. Don set his shoulders and headed for the Steelfab stand, while Jamie turned and headed back towards the main entrance.

3

Outside, it was the most stunning summer's day. Jamie took his jacket off, loosened his tie, threw his jacket over his shoulder held on one finger, and started walking. He walked more quickly than if he were on a stroll; he needed to get somewhere quiet, and quickly. The warm weather had brought a lot of people outside, some in groups and some on their own. A few were lying on open patches of well-tended lawn, apparently asleep; others were reading books on benches, all escaping from the bustle of the exhibition hall for a brief period to make the most of the sunshine. Jamie, head down, just kept walking.

He eventually left the NEC grounds and could hear the motorway in the distance; he didn't want to go that far. Ahead was the beginnings of farmers' fields, and he could see a stile over a fence. He took it, jumping over easily, being careful not to get his clothes dirty—a new challenge since he had left the overalls days behind. He slowed to a more normal walking pace and looked around. He was now following along the side of a tall hedge and had no idea where it would take him. It didn't matter; he would go as far as he needed and then simply turn round and come back.

His mind went back to the conversation he had had with Don Caravello. He had known Don's eldest daughter, Emily, wasn't actually Don's and that he had inherited her when he married Natalie. Hearing that she was the result of a tryst at this show just over sixteen years ago had Jamie worried. If Natalie was his lovely, sweet Bad Penny, then could Emily be his daughter?

He needed to work out the years. He tried to remember how many years in a row he and Penny had met up—was it three ... or maybe four? Bugger it, he couldn't remember. One of the side effects of the ECT shock therapy was this wretched memory loss. Sometimes it came back, sometimes it didn't—and, of course, sometimes you didn't want it to come back. He cursed the treatment now as he tried to remember each of their meetings, but the more he tried to remember, the more jumbled it became in his mind and the more panicked he felt. He needed to calm down.

Another stile over a fence appeared and, instead of climbing over it, he turned and sat down on the step part after brushing off a couple of loose twigs. He was now facing back the way he had come, so he knew he was alone. Feeling the warmth of the wood through his trousers, he laid his jacket over his knees and took a deep breath. All he could hear was birds twittering and the distant rumble of the motorway. There was absolutely no one around; he could take his time now and try to work things out, uninterrupted.

He tried another tack. He knew the year he'd joined Haywood's and was pretty sure that from then, it had been four consecutive years of meeting Penny. Then, on his fingers so as not to lose count, he ticked off the intervening years. Shit—it was seventeen.

He must be Emily's father.

He found himself breathing deeply as he tried to reconcile this possibility in his mind. Who would know? Possibly just her mother, and now him. Did Don know—had Penny told him? Jamie didn't get the sense that he knew; surely there would have been a different vibe between them?

Did it matter? This sixteen-year-old girl had clearly had a good upbringing, almost certainly a lot better than he could ever have offered her—stable parents, a good income, which in turn probably meant a good education and the support of a loving family. He nodded to himself. Don, he felt sure, would have been a good father, so no, it didn't matter.

Then he turned his mind to the big one: did he want to do anything about it, make a claim on her? He needed to think what was best for Emily as well as for himself. Okay, he might gain a daughter, but at what cost? He could break up the happy family that he had just finished praising; he could affect Emily at a sensitive time in her life; and he could set himself back years. He also liked the fact that Penny had been a part of his earlier life, before his problems; they were happy memories, and he wanted to keep them that way. He felt sure that bringing her back into his life after seventeen years would ruin what they once had—and what he dined out on in his mind so often.

Jamie stood up and brushed down the back of his trousers to remove anything loose from the stile. No, he would keep this to himself and not act on it. At the very most, he would observe from a distance by periodically asking Don how his family were. This, he decided, was the best plan all round.

Feeling relieved that he had resolved it in his mind, at least enough to carry on with the day, he picked up his jacket and set off back towards the NEC.

FaB-Ex '12

1

It had become almost a tradition now: curry at their favourite Indian restaurant in the city on the evening of Day 1 at FaB-Ex. Jamie realised he wasn't even sure of the name of the place. He looked at the menu—'Tandoori Temple'; he felt certain it wasn't called that last year. The restaurant was full, which was always a good sign, and the Haywood's group had been lucky to get a table at short notice.

This year, Jamie had asked every Haywood's employee to attend the show for the whole of Day 1 and stay for the meal in the evening. It was then up to them whether they stayed the night or went home, so they had the freedom to have a couple of drinks if they wanted. FaB-Ex had been a major factor in the company's history and growth, so it made sense to have a company meal during the show. It had been a good day, too, with plenty of new business and opportunities presenting themselves. Jamie couldn't be happier.

There were ten of them round the table at the Temple, and for a couple of reasons this was a special year both for the company and for Jamie. Down at the far end of the table, and purposely not sitting next to him, was Josh. Now sixteen, Josh had achieved the results he needed in his final exams and had started his first year at the local technical college. Chilly and Ward had subsequently interviewed him for the position of apprentice fitter with Haywood's.

Jamie had asked Ward to be honest with him: if Josh wasn't suitable, he needed Ward to say so and not simply take him on because he was Jamie's son. Ward had assured Jamie that he would; they had known each other long enough to trust one another to do the right thing.

At the back of his mind, Jamie also worried that the young man might have inherited his mental afflictions and insecurities. Although Chilly and Ward didn't say anything, he felt sure that they too would have been looking for tell-tale signs of this. He knew Chilly wouldn't pull any punches with Josh and would be totally honest with him on his suitability for the position.

The morning after Josh's interview, both Ward and Chilly had avoided eye contact with Jamie and wouldn't mention the interview to him. Jamie, bursting to know how he had got on, had then felt the butterflies in his stomach when he picked up the negative vibes. He needn't have worried: the two of them were winding him up, and they left it until mid morning before breaking the news to Jamie that Josh was more than ready for the Haywood's apprenticeship.

'You bastards!' Jamie had laughed, so relieved, while Ward and Chilly roared with laughter at him.

'You should've seen your face,' Chilly had teased. 'That was just so easy!'

As Jamie looked down the table at Josh sitting at the far end, talking to last year's apprentices, he was full of pride. Will and Dinesh had accepted Josh into the group, and he had been put under Chilly's charge for training. Jamie remembered his own apprenticeship with Chilly and the fun they had had out on the road and at shows. To some extent, he was envious of Josh. He had his whole life ahead of him, and Jamie hoped he made good decisions and took opportunities as and when they were presented to him.

Jamie was aware that as the company MD, he couldn't afford to show Josh any favouritism. When at work, he needed to treat him as any other employee. He had sat Josh down and had a good chat with him about this. There was a lot of shoulder-shrugging on the young man's part; Josh apparently hadn't even considered this happening, let alone seen it as a potential problem. Josh made his own way to work from both his mother's house or Jamie's apartment, and Jamie barely saw him at the office, so separation was actually easy to maintain.

Josh was a well-rounded young man who enjoyed what he did and took his training very seriously. Jamie was pleased to see that he had some good friends at tech college, and they tended to get together and do sports and community activities rather than just go drinking or play online games. Josh interacted well with the people around him too, something both Jamie and Alison had talked about; both had tried to make sure that he was confident in group situations, the unspoken thought being that they didn't want him to struggle like his father.

There were other reasons for this meal being special. Bob had said that he was going to call it a day at Christmas and retire fully from working life. Jamie suspected that Bob would find it hard to do and that they would continue to see him well into the new year; he felt sure Bob would find reasons to come in. Bob's wife had been the driving force behind this, and Jamie had finally accepted that the time had come for him to bow out.

Chilly, too, would be finishing up in the next few months, probably just after Christmas. His retirement, though, unlike Bob's, was driven by his doctor, who had said that he needed to remove all stress from his life and watch his blood pressure and cholesterol levels. This meal certainly wouldn't help in that regard.

Jamie would miss them dearly, but would still see them both on a regular basis outside of work.

The last change was that Haywood's Installations was becoming Haywood & Partners, which would be shortened on the company logo and paperwork to simply 'H&P'. It was time to make the move from a small family business to a more corporate image.

The ten around the table were made up of the three apprentices at the far end; Bob, Ward, Chilly and Jamie; Gerry, the fitter who had been with them just under a year; Peter, who was in charge of stores, tools and hardware; and Lydia, the receptionist and secretary who was also Peter's wife. They were a good tight team, and Jamie knew he was fortunate to have such a good team. However, with Bob and Chilly leaving, they would be down to eight. Ward would step up to fill the gap left by Chilly and had been given the title of operations manager, which he was delighted with..

The biggest gap was going to be left by Bob, who did all the sales and marketing. He was a natural, plus he had all the contacts and knew all the customers personally, having worked with them for years. He was completely comfortable visiting new companies who were interested in the company's services or giving presentations in front of large groups of people. Jamie had never been good at this, even before his darkness had descended. He was essentially a shy man, and while he was a good engineer, he was not a natural sales person. Taking on the company's sales and marketing activities would stretch him and was sure to put him out of his comfort zone, which concerned him greatly from a health point of view.

The first drinks had now been delivered around the table and the food orders taken. Jamie picked up his knife and tapped the side of his glass to attract everyone's attention.

'Ladies and gentlemen,' he started, before correcting himself, looking at Lydia along the table, 'or maybe I should say "Lady and gentlemen"?'

He became aware that not only were all nine people in front of him now watching him intently, but so were people sitting at the tables around him. Suddenly self-conscious, he felt the panic rise and his palms and forehead became sweaty.

'Yeah, Jamie!' Chilly shouted and slapped him on the back. 'Our MD is going to give us a rousing inspirational speech.'

Jamie smiled. Chilly was right: he was the new MD, he had chosen this position for himself, these nine people were looking to him for leadership, and now was his time to do just that. He cleared this throat, looked round the table and carried on.

'No speech, I promise you—just to say "thank you" to all of you for being here today, and tonight. I appreciate you are all away from your families. Also a huge thank-you for the work you all put in every day for Haywood's—H&P,' he corrected himself. 'That's going to take some getting used to. A company is only as good as its employees, and I know better than anyone that we all have strengths and weaknesses, but if we work together we become stronger than the sum of our individual abilities. I think it's called synergy.'

'Boring!' Chilly slapped him on the back again. It was what Jamie needed as he felt himself struggling to get to the point.

Feeling more relaxed after Chilly's heckle, Jamie smiled and added, 'Oh, and one more thing I'll be doing—which I wish Bob had done twenty years ago.' He paused as Bob tried to work out what could be coming. 'I'll be investing in our own vacuum cleaners. I'm fed up of having to borrow bloody vacuum cleaners off other stands.'

A laugh went round the table as all eyes turned to Bob, who gave him the thumbs-up. As silence returned and everyone looked back at him, Jamie raised his glass.

'My point is ... Thank you—all of you. I know that H&P is in good hands.'

Bob, Ward and Chilly started whooping, Jamie felt his back being slapped again, and all raised their glasses in his direction. It had been a bit clumsy, but he had given his first company speech as the new Managing Director of Haywood and Partners.

FaB-Ex '13

1

From his vantage point on the H&P booth Jamie saw Bradley Copchase enter Hall 3. Bradley had his head down and walked briskly past without looking up. Jamie was ready to say hello and wave, but he wasn't given the opportunity.

It was just Jamie and Ward on the stand at that moment. It was Day 3 and they were expecting it to be busy. Or hoping it would be busy—the show had been quieter than normal this year, and there weren't as many exhibitors as usual. Jamie guessed that budgets were tight these days and companies were questioning the amount of money spent on exhibition stands. It was often difficult to gauge the value of the money spent at expos like this. If a company doesn't have a stand, its absence is noticed, but having one involves a huge financial outlay, which is hard to justify. Most companies wrote it off as a necessary evil.

Jamie's mind went back to Bradley Copchase and the fact that he still hadn't made his peace with him. Why not now—what did he have to lose? It was overdue.

He walked across to Ward, who was standing with his hands behind his back, trying not to look bored. 'Once the boys are back, do you mind if I shoot off for a few minutes?'

'Course not, no. Don't wait for the boys; if you have to go, just go.' Ward was as accommodating as ever.

Jamie decided to tell him. 'I think the time has come for me to formally apologise to Bradley and Wallace Copchase.'

'Really?' Ward seemed surprised. 'Would you like me to come with you?'

'No, but thanks. I think it would look better if I go along on my own—less cowardly, somehow.'

At that moment, the three apprentices appeared back on the stand, each carrying white plastic bags full of brochures and leaflets picked off other stands.

'No excuse now,' Ward smiled. 'Say hello to the smarmy bastard from me, won't you?'

Jamie gave him a rueful smile. 'I will, thanks,' He turned to Josh, Will and Dinesh. 'You guys okay? Do you mind sticking round until I get back? Help Ward out.'

The three apprentices seemed delighted with the sudden, though temporary, promotion to sales.

'Yeah, no problem, Jamie,' Will said. He seemed to have become the spokesman for the apprentice group. He then said to Dinesh and Josh, 'Hopefully those girls will walk by again,' and in explanation to Ward and Jamie, 'One of the girls on a stand in Hall 5 has taken a bit of a liking to your Josh.'

All three boys giggled, but Ward felt that he needed to be the voice of authority.

'Don't forget you're supposed to be working here this week—this isn't a bloody pick-up joint.' All three nodded back at Ward, who winked to Jamie after the reprimand.

Jamie set off. It would only take a minute to get to the Steelfab stand, which was just a little further down the first aisle. He didn't mind leaving the stand. Ward was far better at dealing with prospective customers than he was, although he was improving, but it didn't come naturally to him. He loved the day-to-day running of the business and had settled into it well; he was a natural organiser, and the employees seemed to trust him. There was no doubt, though, that sales and marketing were his weaknesses, and as the company grew, this was becoming more and more obvious. Ward was happy to visit prospective customer sites to give talks and presentations, but it meant him being away from his own job for a day, something Jamie was very aware of and needed to do something about.

As he walked onto the Steelfab stand, he realised that he hadn't prepared a speech—he didn't know what he was going to say to Bradley or Wallace.

Bradley was at the back of the stand and had watched him approach. He was with two other men and had said something to them surreptitiously as Jamie came up to him. Bradley's eyes were wide as Jamie approached, but he didn't speak. He looked wary, nervous even.

Still not sure what to say, Jamie raised a hand in a gesture of friendship and said simply, 'I'm sorry, Bradley, I owe you and Wallace an apology for my behaviour a few years ago.'

Bradley slowly raised his hand and took Jamie's, shaking it slowly and briefly. Jamie noticed that his hand was clammy—was this normal, or was he nervous? Bradley still didn't speak, and the two men on either side of him now looked like his own personal bodyguards.

'Where is Wallace?' Jamie continued. 'I would like to apologise in person.'

'Wallace doesn't work with us any more,' Bradley finally answered. 'He left a few years back.'

'Ah. Okay. Where is he now?' Jamie tried to keep the stilted conversation going.

'He does industrial design work; works in a large open-plan office somewhere in Manchester.'

'Is he happy—is he enjoying it? Was that his choice?' Jamie was genuinely intrigued to know if Wallace had jumped or if he had been pushed.

'Loves it,' Bradley replied. 'Said he thought expos like this were dangerous places—he kept getting beaten up.'

Was Bradley trying to be funny, or was this simply a dig? Jamie would tread cautiously. 'Well, please pass on my apology to him. I mean it; I sincerely regret what I did.'

Bradley nodded, and Jamie thought he saw the flicker of a smile. 'Thank you, Jamie,' he said, 'I will let him know. I heard later you were ... having difficulties at the time.'

Jamie nodded. Perhaps it was time to go; he had said his piece, and there had been no unpleasantness. But Bradley hadn't quite finished.

'It was Don who told me, Don Caravello—our ex-sales manager? Obviously thought a lot of you at the time—stood up for you, and then had a go at Wallace himself a year or two later, I believe.'

Jamie wasn't sure what to say. 'Yes, I heard about that.' He didn't want to get involved in that mix-up as well. 'Where is Don now? I haven't seen him here this year.'

Bradley puffed up a little bit as he answered. 'I don't know and I don't care,' he said aggressively. 'Mind you, I did hear he was going through a personal issue at the moment, so maybe he's off work for a bit.'

'Personal issue?'

'I'm told his wife died a month or two back.'

Jamie felt his mouth open and his eyes widen. 'What ...? No!'

'Natalie,' Bradley continued. 'Lovely girl. Breast cancer, apparently. Leaves Don with two teenage girls to look after; I think the eldest just turned eighteen.'

For the first time in a number of years, Jamie felt the darkness descending on him and the world started to close in around him. Noises became jumbled and confused, and he lost the sharpness to his peripheral vision. He couldn't think of anything to say and turned to walk off the stand, raising his hand in a gesture of goodbye. He felt physically sick.

As he headed back along the walkway, Jamie pulled out his wallet and unclasped it, then stepped to one side out of the flow of people. On the right-hand side of the wallet, opposite his business cards, was a small zipped compartment that he hardly ever opened. It contained a few artefacts that he liked to keep on him at all times. There was a picture of Josh as a baby, the first picture ever taken of him. Below that was a gold coin with St Christopher on, which his mum had bought him when he first started travelling for his job; she said it would keep him safe.

He dug further and pulled out two much-folded pieces of paper, one inside the other. Both were on Novotel letterhead, stained and dog-eared from years of handling: the two notes left for him by beautiful Penny nearly twenty years ago.

He hadn't seen her in years, but she was always a presence in his mind, a reminder of everything that was good in the world, a representation of happy memories and a time in his life when he was carefree and had no responsibilities.

But she was gone. His dear Bad Penny wouldn't be coming back any more.

FaB-Ex '14

1

Business was booming again. More and more equipment manufacturers were looking to outsource their sitework and installations rather than have their own employees potentially sitting round between jobs, and H&P had gained a reputation for excellence. Their attention to detail and thoroughness in completing jobs was well recognised in the industry. Jamie genuinely believed that this was a result of Bob and Chilly's influence on the fitters and apprentices during their training.

Both Will and Dinesh had completed their apprenticeships now and were qualified technicians. Josh would graduate in the next couple of months and would also become an H&P fitter, able to go out on jobs on his own.

From the back of the booth Jamie watched Josh talking to one of the operators from a recent install at a toothpaste factory, who had been having difficulties with the throughput. Jamie was very proud of his son but didn't want to show it. Josh seemed to know what he was talking about, and he clearly had a good rapport with this particular operator.

He had grown into a nice-looking young man too. He had short dark hair and was stocky in stature with kind eyes and a warm smile. Jamie could see himself in Josh, but also elements of Alison, too—he certainly had his mother's confidence and interpersonal skills. Perhaps he had inherited the best of both of them: Jamie's temperament, looks and attitude and Alison's outgoing nature and strength of character.

Ward came across to speak to Jamie and noticed he was watching his son.

'He's doing well, Jamie, he'll go a long way.' Jamie nodded. 'Have you thought that this company may be too small for him? Maybe he should get a job somewhere else, broaden his experiences ... I don't know—go overseas, work for a big multinational for a while? Then he could make his own mind up as to whether he wants to come back to H&P.'

The same idea had crossed Jamie's mind. He didn't want to push Josh to take over from him at some point in the future, but if he did end up taking the reins, that would be the ultimate for a father. However, he too wanted his son to experience some of the world, come out from under his father's shadow and to be able to spread his wings.

'I've thought of that, too,' he said. 'Once he's out of the apprenticeship, I might have a chat with him, see if he's interested; then if he is, perhaps I could have a word with the Jacobs guys—see if they could offer him a placement somewhere, maybe as a project engineer.'

'That's a great idea,' Ward confirmed. The two of them looked back at Josh, who was just finishing up with the operator. They noticed a girl standing just beyond the pair, just off the stand, and both assumed she must be connected to the toothpaste man.

'Have you thought any more about taking on someone for sales?' Ward asked.

'I have,' Jamie answered, 'and I think we should. The timing is right at the moment; the industry is growing. There probably isn't enough sales work on its own, but if he knew about marketing as well and could handle the website and social media, it could be quite a good job—broad and challenging.'

'You're not enjoying the salesy stuff, are you?'

'Hating it,' Jamie answered with a smile. 'I've never been into this social media stuff—I think I missed the rush when it all became the rage. I don't even have a Facebook account. Leave that to the younger generation.'

They both looked back towards Josh, and to their surprise he had his arms around the girl who had been waiting patiently in the walkway.

'All grown up, eh? How old is he now—eighteen?' Ward asked as the two men watched.

Jamie smiled back at him without speaking and tried not to stare at the young couple, so happy in each other's arms. Their eyes were locked on each other's, and she was whispering something that only he would be able to hear.

Watching the scene took Jamie back over twenty years to his first few visits to FaB-Ex and the excitement of a pretty girl. He had been Billy-no-mates and she was the Bad Penny, but it had been fun, a lot of fun. He felt a stab of pain as he remembered that she was no longer here. Gone too soon ... What was it they said—'only the good die young'? Wasn't that a song too? He pictured her face, dazzlingly pretty with such a beautiful smile. He remembered how he had shouted at her on the Steelfab stand and how, rather than get angry with him for it, she immediately understood and forgave him.

Had she been responsible for his darkness descending, or had her memory helped to get him through it? He didn't know, and never would. What he was sure of was that his life had been richer for those few brief encounters he had shared with her. The feeling of pain was still there, and he knew from the last twelve months that it would take a while to pass. Finding out about her death at the previous FaB-Ex had hurt him much worse than he would have imagined. In his mind, he had put her on a pedestal—the perfect human being, the perfect partner. Would it have ever worked out between them, had they stayed together? Again, he would never know, but he liked to think so.

While Jamie had been reminiscing, Ward had moved away to speak to a couple of men who were standing just off the booth, leaving Jamie on his own. Josh walked over to his dad, pulling the girl along with him by the hand. She looked coy and shy. Jamie tried to clear his mind and put a warm welcoming smile on his face. He wasn't good at hiding his apprehension at first meetings with new people, but he was getting better with practice.

'Hello,' he offered, looking directly at the attractive young lady. 'I'm Jamie.'

'Hello, Jamie,' she replied, surprisingly confidently. 'I'm Emily, Emily Caravello.'

2

Jamie was very aware that he had acted strangely when he had first met Emily. He had put on a brave face and excused himself, walking away with a smile. Josh might possibly have realised that something was wrong, but he doubted Emily would have noticed.

And now here he was, back at his stile in the Warwickshire countryside, somewhere between the NEC and the M42 motorway, trying to get things straight in his mind again.

Did he need to worry? What did he need to worry about? Was he shocked because he may have just met his own nineteen-year-old daughter, or was he frightened that she seemed to be his eighteen-year-old son's girlfriend? His mind was doing somersaults. He couldn't get the facts to settle in an order that he could deal with them.

He had now had three years to come to terms with the fact that he had a daughter and twelve months with the fact that her mother had died. He had assumed that he would never meet her, that she would always be Don and Natalie Caravello's eldest daughter; but he *had* met her. Like her mother, she looked perfect, a beautiful young lady with character and presence. Jamie sighed. Oh shit, what had he done, and what should he do?

It wasn't as warm on the stile as when he had sat here three years before on that sunny afternoon. He forced himself to think about his predicament. What about the fact that Emily was seeing Josh? At what point did he break it to his son that he was going out with his own sister?

'Shit, shit, shit!' He said it out loud, but thankfully there was no one near to hear him. An answer wasn't presenting itself to him this time. He just didn't know what to do.

For the moment, though, he needed to get a grip. He was the company's managing director in the middle of its biggest exhibition of the year. His staff were looking to him for guidance, leadership and strength—and so was his son. Jamie decided that he needed to get back to the booth and that he would try his best to push the issue to one side for now; hopefully he could deal with it once the show was over. He wasn't good at compartmentalising his personal problems. He could do it with work issues, no problem, and jump from one current challenge to another, but his personal problems were a different matter.

Perhaps he just simply needed to tell Josh the truth—perhaps it was time for it all to come out? Maybe he couldn't hide his secret any more. What did he have to be ashamed of? After all, he had only found out about Emily when she was a teenager.

He hadn't made a good first impression with her, though—in fact, he had been on the verge of being rude, and for Josh's sake he needed to correct that.

He hopped off the stile and dusted himself down. Despite thinking he couldn't resolve this issue, he had made a tough decision and had a plan.

3

When Jamie got back to the booth, Emily was still there, just outside on the main walkway carpet, talking to Will and Dinesh. Josh, meanwhile, was talking to a customer in the booth and seemed fully absorbed.

Seeing Jamie approaching, the three youngsters all straightened up and stopped chatting. The two young fitters liked Jamie, but he was still their superior and as the company figurehead, he deserved respect.

'Excuse me, guys,' he said, 'do you mind if I have a chat with Emily?' The two young men shrugged and moved away. Emily didn't react, and Jamie waited until the two lads were out of earshot, further along the stand.

'Can I have a chat with you?' he asked. 'Perhaps we can walk. Do you fancy a cup of tea?'

Emily nodded, not sure what was going on or what to expect. Jamie glanced back at the stand, but Josh had his back to them and was still talking to a man in a suit. The two of them started to walk away from the booth in the direction of the coffee shop, Jamie setting the pace as a slow plod so that he had time to talk to her. He had decided that he needed to be honest with her and launched straight in.

'Emily, I'm sorry if I reacted strangely earlier, when Josh introduced you.' She nodded politely, it was clear that she *had* thought that his reaction was odd. 'I used to know your mum,' he said, 'and I was really sorry to hear she lost her battle.'

'That's okay,' she answered quietly. 'People don't know what to say to me even if they didn't know my mum, so I understand it must have been weird for you. When did you know her?'

How much did Jamie tell her? Maybe he needed to tread cautiously for the moment, but he felt sure he could talk about her without going too far at this stage.

'I first met her when she was a Wow! girl,' Jamie said, the memory making him smile, 'right here actually, at FaB-Ex. It was the first year I came here. I was an apprentice at the time, working for this same company.'

'Is that right?' Emily seemed really interested. 'So you knew her before my dad?'

'I guess so.' Jamie needed to tread very carefully now, but the young girl just wanted to hear about her mum.

'What was she like?'

Choosing his words cautiously, Jamie heard himself say, 'She was lovely, a real character. One of the most genuine people I have ever met—beautiful inside and out.' He felt himself starting to well up and needed to stop talking.

'I've heard that,' Emily said. 'She used to talk about her Wow! days like it was one long party.'

Jamie wanted to change the subject slightly. 'How's your dad?' he asked.

They had reached the coffee shop, and for once there was no queue. Jamie mouthed, 'Tea?' at her and she nodded as she answered. 'He was really bad initially—we all were—but he's getting it together now.'

'Is he back at work?'

'Yes, went back after a few months. Gloucester's were really good and told him to take as long as he needed, but I think he needed the distraction.'

'I'm so sorry, Emily,' Jamie said. 'I know your dad well, too; he's always been very good to me, and I owe him a lot. I'm sorry to hear he's been in the wars. What a terrible thing for anyone to have to go through.'

The tea arrived in a stainless steel pot, with two mugs, a small jug of milk, and four sachets of sugar.

'Looks like a self-assembly job, doesn't it?' Jamie quipped.

'You'll be good at that, then.' Emily laughed at her own joke. 'So I'll let you assemble it.'

Jamie decided he liked this girl, really liked her. He studied her features hard and couldn't see either himself or Penny in her. There were no obviously inherited features, but sometimes they don't always stand out.

He poured the tea while Emily talked.

'My dad didn't really have any hobbies outside of work, so the problem was that once he came home from work and at the weekends, he just used to sink into depression. He would spend all his time thinking about Mum, and it wasn't doing him any good. He was making himself worse.'

Jamie noticed a tear in the corner of her eye and offered her a tissue, but she waved it away and dabbed her eye. Jamie added milk and sugar to his tea, stirred it and offered them to Emily, but again she waved them away.

'I was busy trying to hold Laura together—my little sister—so poor Dad used to go off on his own.'

Jamie sighed. He thought a lot of Don, and hated to think of him going through this.

'Then he made a decision a few months ago,' she continued. 'He decided that instead of moping around, wasting his time feeling sorry for himself, he would start the Natalie Caravello Foundation. And now he spends all his spare time working on that. It gives him something to do and, in a strange way, it makes him feel like he's closer to her again.' Emily took a mouthful of her tea, but it was still hot and she winced.

'What does the foundation do?' Jamie asked. He saw her visibly grow in front of him; it was clearly something she was very proud of.

'It's a charity. We fund research and equipment for the breast cancer programs at the hospital Mum died in.'

Jamie smiled at her. This girl had been through a lot and had come out of the other end with her head held high and a smile on her face. He couldn't tell her; the last thing she needed right now was another bombshell.

For all the wrong reasons, he really hoped that she and Josh would break up.

FaB-Ex '15

1

Jamie was on the H&P stand first and had laid out the brochures and business cards. This year, for the first time, they were pushing their servicing and maintenance facility, and they had a slightly larger booth—probably a 'stand' now, rather than a 'booth', with a couple of display tables positioned at the front. Jamie opened the locked cupboard under one of the tables and took out a gearbox and some mechanical seals, laying them out neatly on the table above, along with the sign saying what they were. He went out onto the walkway carpet and looked back at them. They looked great.

He pulled his laptop out of his bag and returned the bag to the locked cabinet, turning the key securely. He had heard of a lot of incidents of theft at these shows in recent years, and even though they were right at the front and under a CCTV camera, he didn't want to take the risk. He remembered the incident at the show right at the beginning of his career—that time, the police had reckoned it was an organised gang targeting specific stands—and how the incident had led him to meet up with Penny in the security office. His mood lightened as he thought of her. Funny how he had seen her every year for four years and then never again. In a strange way, even after twenty years, he missed her still.

He opened his laptop. He needed to kill off his emails as his first job, put them to one side before Day 1 started. He had worked out that today would be twenty-five years since his first show, the one he had come to with Chilly as a young apprentice, the one at which he first met Penny. He shook his head. He had to stop reminiscing; there would be time for that later, and of course there was the traditional Indian meal for the whole company at the Tandoori Temple this evening. He was looking forward to that, but today would be a busy day, and he had a lot on—and not all of it was work related.

Jamie still hadn't said anything to Josh or Emily. Despite really liking her, he hoped beyond hope that they would break up. As far as he knew, Emily was Josh's first crush and first love, and as such he had hoped that they would grow apart after the initial obsession period. But it hadn't happened—quite the opposite, in fact.

Jamie had barely seen Josh this past year. He had decided some time ago that there wasn't enough room at his father's apartment and had moved into the spare room at Alison and David's, where he had more space and independence. They were happy with this arrangement as it meant they had a built-in house-sitter if they wanted to go away for the weekend. Jamie saw Josh at work from time to time, and they spent the odd day together at weekends. Jamie didn't see much of Emily, certainly not as much as he wanted.

Then, back in June, Josh had moved out of Alison and David's and into a shared studio apartment with Emily. Jamie had hoped that living together would bring out each other's flaws that might drive them apart, but apparently that wasn't the case, as a few weeks ago Josh had announced that they were engaged. Jamie had done his best to look pleased, but it had thrown him into turmoil. The time had come to tell them, but he needed to tell both of them together and face to face.

Emily still worked for the same company as her stepfather, Don, in a junior sales role. She was a fixture now on the Gloucester Process Solutions stand at FaB-Ex, so he knew he would see her this week. Jamie had checked with Josh, who had confirmed that they were driving up together. Today was the day: he would get them together at lunchtime and tell them. It would break their hearts, and the thought of doing it made him feel physically sick, but he had to do it. He had images of grandchildren with webbed feet.

He took a deep breath—one thing at a time—and opened his emails. There were a lot that he had simply been copied on, and he read these quickly and moved on. He looked at his watch: 9.50 am. Ward and all the others would be here soon, and in the hall there was an air of apprehension ahead of the FaB-Ex show opening at 10 am.

There was an email from Ward about the recent first interviews for the sales position. They needed a candidate with both sales and marketing experience, ideally within a smaller business, and had struggled to find someone suitable. Everyone who had come forward so far was either strongly sales or strongly marketing, and the few that demonstrated both were simply too expensive for their small company. Ward's email confirmed that he had interviewed three more candidates and had since rung them all to let them go. On the phone the day before, Ward had described them as a fuckwit, a dandy and a smug bastard. Ward was a good judge of character, and Jamie trusted his opinion; he knew that if someone made it through to interview with him—the MD—they would be a very strong candidate indeed.

Surely, there must be someone out there. Jamie was considering the unthinkable: putting the search in the hands of a recruitment agency. They were a profession that Jamie had never thought much of, but the search was starting to take up too much of his and Ward's time, and he would need to bite the bullet and outsource it. They needed someone badly—the website was in desperate need of a revamp, new enquiries were going unanswered and their social media presence was non-existent.

There was a reply email to Ward's from Lydia, the company receptionist, to say that a new candidate, Sam Warren, had come forward ... Sam would be at FaB-Ex in the afternoon and would drop by to discuss the role and present a proposal to them ... Sam's cover letter and CV were attached.

Typical bloody salesman, Jamie thought, *always has a proposal*. He knew that Lydia's workload was increasing and that finding someone to fill the sales position would be a great help to her also. He dropped her a quick line of thanks and said he would look at the letter and CV later.

He saw Ward and a group of the young fitters—Josh included—walking towards him through the main entry doors. He waved at them, and they all waved back. Ward reached the stand with a heavy sigh, and dropped his bag down by the table.

'Here we go again,' he said, 'like Groundhog Day.' Jamie tossed him the key for the lockable cupboard, and Ward went to lock his briefcase away. Jamie crossed to where the three young fitters were admiring the gearbox on the tabletop.

'Morning, guys,' he said. They all acknowledged him, and he turned to Josh. 'Joshy, is Em here today?'

'Yes, she's on the Gloucester's stand all day,' he said. 'Why?'

'Could she get away for an hour or so? I'd like to buy you both lunch.' He paused and could already feel the butterflies in his stomach. 'And there's something I would like to talk to you both about.'

'Sure, I'll tell her. She'll be delighted. She said she had something for you, anyway.'

Jamie barely heard him. He had set it up now; there was no going back.

2

Jamie had asked to meet Josh and Emily at the restaurant off the Piazza, rather than the coffee shop, as he needed somewhere quieter and less public for what he had to tell them. He couldn't believe the pain he was about to inflict on these two young people, two people who simply didn't deserve this ... his own flesh and blood. He also couldn't believe what a coward he had been; he should have told them long ago, a year ago, before it all became so serious. They would both have moved on by now.

He had found a table against the far wall and took the seat looking into the restaurant. Jamie always sat with his back to the wall, a throwback to his days of paranoia and a habit he couldn't get out of. In this case, though, it was a conscious decision so he could see them coming in.

In his mind, he had worked out his speech and rehearsed it over and over. He just needed to say it and had decided he would do it first up. The lunch might never happen as a result, but he couldn't sit through the whole meal knowing what he had to do.

He saw them walk in, and they spotted him immediately. Josh smiled, and Emily ran over and gave him a hug. He adored this girl. She had a plastic bag in her hand, which she placed carefully against a table leg.

Jamie had pre-ordered a round of drinks, as he knew what they would have: a Coke for Josh and a lime soda for Emily. Jamie had ordered himself a whisky—he would need it.

The drinks arrived as they all sat down, and Jamie immediately took a big mouthful without thinking. The young lovers would have assumed this was a celebration lunch for their engagement, something Jamie only realised as he saw their faces watching him take his mouthful. In a strange moment, Jamie found himself apologising and raising his glass to them.

'To Josh and Emily,' he said. They both raised their glasses slightly and thanked him. Emily kept glancing at Josh; something was going on—*Oh, God, tell me she's not pregnant!*

'I have something I need to tell you,' Jamie started. Here goes: it was time for the pre-prepared speech. He cleared his throat in readiness.

'No, no. Me first, me first!' Emily was excited and could barely contain herself. She jumped about in her seat, her eyes bright as she looked back and forth between Josh and Jamie.

Oh Christ, she *was* pregnant. Jamie knew it. He'd left it too late. He felt the dark mist gathering above him, and his peripheral vision began to blur. His palms were sweating. He looked at Josh, but he didn't seem anywhere near as excited—not as excited as an expectant father should be. Perhaps the thought of fatherhood didn't appeal to him?

Emily reached down and picked up the plastic bag. Jamie was panicking. Was this going to be the ultrasound image of his grandchild? Did webbed feet show up at this early stage? He felt the beads of sweat forming on his forehead as Emily pulled a picture frame out of the plastic bag, initially with its back facing toward Jamie.

'My dad—Don,' she corrected herself, '... wanted to give you this, but I begged him to let me do it.'

She pulled the bag away completely and dropped it onto the floor. Jamie thought he heard her voice check, as if she was about to cry.

'This is a thank-you ... from us—my dad, my sister and me—for all the generous donations Haywood's have made to the Natalie Caravello Foundation.'

This wasn't what Jamie had been expecting. A year ago he had asked Lydia to set up a monthly donation to the Natalie Caravello Foundation—partly because he felt it was a good cause, partly because he felt it would go some way to repaying Don, and partly out of a sense of ongoing commitment to his beloved Penny. He hadn't really been involved in it, apart from authorising the monthly payments.

'Honestly, Em,' he stumbled, 'it's the least we can do, it's a great cause, and we're happy to—'

Jamie stopped mid sentence as Emily turned the frame around to face him.

It was an A4 certificate in a handsome wooden frame, with a photograph and some text below it, which read

An expression of gratitude for the generosity of
Haywood and Partners Ltd
for their ongoing and generous contributions to the Natalie
Caravello Foundation

Below the text were three signatures, which he assumed were those of Don, Emily and Laura. Taking up pride of place in the centre was a head-and-shoulders photograph of a beautiful woman. She was smiling for the camera and, ironically, looked full of life. Written across the photo in a stylised font was

Natalie Caravello

But the woman was blonde. She wasn't Penny.

Jamie was dumbstruck and slowly reached across the table to take the frame out of Emily's hands. 'That's your mum?' he almost whispered.

'Yes,' she answered, dabbing the corners of her eyes with her napkin and taking a small mouthful of her drink. 'You said you knew her?'

Jamie, gathering his thoughts, was thankful that he was able to hide behind the framed gift.

'It's beautiful ...' he mumbled, '... she's beautiful ... thank you ... thank you so much.'

It wasn't Bad Penny. Natalie Caravello wasn't his dear Penny. How could this be? How could he have got it so wrong? He looked at the woman in the photo more closely.

He did know her, though. In his mind he pictured her saying, 'Really?'

Of course! This was the girl Penny had been with the night they first met. The two girls had stayed in the bar at the hotel after the others had left, and then the blonde one—the woman he now knew to be Natalie—had gone off to a nightclub in the city on her own.

Jamie had hidden behind the frame for long enough, and he gently lowered it, being careful not to knock over the glasses on the table. 'Thank you, Em, this means a lot to me.'

They would never understand just how much it meant.

3

The meal had taken a very different course from what Jamie had expected. If Natalie Caravello wasn't Penny, then Emily wasn't his daughter, and there was no need to give his speech. Jamie felt like a cloud had lifted from over his head, a cloud that had hung there for over a year. He felt like a free man once again.

Josh and Emily had enjoyed their meals and had talked about redecorating their little studio flat. Jamie had hardly heard a word. His mind had been on Penny and Natalie Caravello, and how they had been two different people all along. The inaccurate fact that they were the same person had been cemented in his mind for so long that he now struggled to recall how he had come to that conclusion in the first place. This one wrong assumption had dictated a lot of his behaviour in recent years: how he had treated Don, and why he had been so scared to attend the meal in town the night Chilly had his heart attack. He genuinely couldn't recall how he had reached that assumption. *Damn the shock therapy*—his memory was vague or tangled at best, especially around things he subconsciously wanted to forget.

He had seen the name on her hotel room bill that one time: 'N Dawson,' which he had later assumed was her maiden name. And then Chilly had found him the business card given to Bob, which confirmed that she was Natalie Caravello. He couldn't understand how he could have got this so wrong?

Later that afternoon, Jamie was back at the coffee shop, a short walk from the H&P stand. He had received a text from this Sam Warren, asking if they could meet there at 3 pm to discuss his sales and marketing requirements. He had come straight from the restaurant, leaving Josh and Emily to go back to their respective company stands. Jamie had almost skipped out of the restaurant; he was on cloud nine and kept looking at the image in the frame to check it was still the same woman. He had wanted to read Sam's letter and CV before the meeting but hadn't had the chance to go back to the stand to get his laptop, so he would just have to wing it. He'd get the meeting out of the way as quickly as possible and get back to help out at the stand. He was now really looking forward to the company meal in a few hours time and hoped he hadn't eaten too much in the restaurant at lunchtime.

He looked at his watch: exactly 3 pm. He looked to left and right; no sign of anyone, but the coffee shop was starting to get busy. It was time for a lot of people to have their mid-afternoon break before the final push towards the end of Day 1. Some were having tea, but most were having their first beer or glass of wine.

Jamie looked out at the hall, spread out in front of him. This place had been such a major part of his life. He had been through serious ups and serious downs here, but for twenty-five years it had been a regular pitstop in his life. He looked down at the floor and mulled over the roller-coaster ride he had been on to get here.

The perfume hit him first, a perfume that he knew. Then he heard a gasp in front of him and brought his mind back to the present and his 3 pm meeting. He looked up. To his surprise, a woman was standing in front of him, not saying anything. She wore a blue-green summery dress and high-heeled shoes. Okay, so Sam wasn't a bloke as he had assumed. He now felt badly that he hadn't had time to read her CV. He stood up and, for the first time, saw her face. He nearly fell back into his seat as his eyes widened in shock and his jaw fell open.

It was Penny. His Bad Penny.

His 3 pm meeting was with his dear, sweet Penny.

Her face was the same but different; she wasn't a girl any more, but a beautiful woman. Her hair was pretty much as he remembered from the last time he had seen her—shoulder-length brunette, but styled. Jamie was aware that he was staring, but then so was she.

Jamie tried to gather himself and closed his mouth, without blinking or taking his eyes off her. He was afraid that she might vanish again or that perhaps he was hallucinating. She managed to compose herself first.

'Billy-no-mates?' she asked.

Jamie smiled, and without thinking gave her the prompt that she needed. 'You're back?'

'Like a bad penny,' she confirmed, adding, 'as my dear old grandma would have said.'

Jamie held out his hand, still not taking his eyes off her. 'Jamie Prescott,' he offered. 'I'm pleased to meet you.'

'Samantha Warren ... Sam,' she replied, taking his hand. Jamie didn't want to let go and now wasn't sure exactly what was appropriate.

With their hands still gripped, she pulled herself towards him and wrapped her arms around him.

'I've missed you,' she said.

'You have no idea,' Jamie answered, his head buried into her neck, 'no idea.'

4

Jamie couldn't recall a time in his life when he had felt so positive. All vestiges of his darkness had lifted, and he was a different person.

He had invited the whole company back again for the traditional Indian meal at the Tandoori Temple—fourteen of them this year, but he had booked a table for fifteen.

Included in the fourteen were Bob and Chilly, whom Jamie had invited for old times' sake, and he was delighted to see them standing in the doorway as he and Ward arrived. The four men greeted each other warmly, and two pints of lager were passed to Jamie and Ward, courtesy of Bob. They chatted for five or ten minutes as the rest of the staff arrived.

At seven o'clock promptly, they were ushered to a long table of the far side of the restaurant, and Jamie, as always, took his seat against the far wall, looking in. On the wall behind him was a large mirror, presumably there to make the restaurant look bigger than it actually was. He caught a glimpse of himself as he sat down, and he wondered where the young man had gone, the young man Sam had met twenty-five years ago. He was fortunate not to have put on much weight over that time and he was still pretty fit, but the tough years were etched onto his face as creases in his forehead and under his eyes. He was going grey above his temples and at the front, and he wondered if what Sam had seen after all those years was a disappointment. He dismissed the thought as best he could and turned away from the mirror to look back into the room.

The table had a 'Reserved' sign on it, which he moved to the seat to his right, explaining to Ward, who was shuffling along towards him, 'Can I keep this seat free, please, Ward? I'm expecting our new sales and marketing manager.'

Ward looked at him, frowned at first and then smiled. 'Really?' he said. 'I'm intrigued. Tell me more.'

Jamie waited while Ward took the seat two away from him, leaving the gap as requested.

'I've decided to outsource. I've found someone who knows the industry well—in fact she's been in it just as long as I have and started her own agency a few years back to service small businesses like ours. For a monthly fee, her company will oversee the website, manage the customer database and do all that social media nonsense.'

'And sales?'

'They represent us as if they were our own sales team—visit sites, do the presentations—but we only pay them if they get an order—a commission. Yet to work out the detail, but it all makes sense to me. I wanted you to meet her first.'

Ward nodded slowly as he digested what Jamie had told him. 'Okay; makes sense, I guess.'

A round of drinks was delivered to each person around the table. Jamie found himself with both a fresh pint and the one he had been handed at the bar, now with only a few mouthfuls left in it. He remembered what Chilly had said to him at the hotel bar, literally seconds before his heart attack. He picked up his old pint and handed it to the waiter.

'That one is done,' he said, 'thank you.' That pint of lager was his life until now. It was time for a fresh start, and he took a big sip from his other glass, savouring its cold crispness, as the waiter took the old one away without question.

As always, the Tandoori Temple was packed, and he was glad he had made a reservation. The full complement were here again, and even the office-bound members of staff like Lydia and Peter were here for the evening, not just for the meal. They had decided to stay this year and would have a couple of drinks with their work colleagues before heading back to the office in the morning.

Jamie had butterflies in his stomach. Would she show, or would she disappear from his life once again? At the coffee shop they had remained in an embrace for a long time, just holding each other. It must have looked very unusual to all the seated patrons around them, but neither had cared. Eventually, they had let go of each other and sat down facing one another, but still holding hands like teenagers. In Jamie's mind, they were still teenagers, yet he was looking into the eyes of a mature woman.

Jamie had fired questions at her. 'But your room bill that time said you were N Dawson? I assumed that was Natalie Dawson and that Dawson must have been your maiden name.'

'It probably did,' she had replied thoughtfully. 'Nat used to book the rooms, so her name was always on the bills for all of us. We used to joke that we could do a runner and she would have to pay for everyone.'

She hadn't changed; she was still the same outgoing, go-get girl that he had met all those years ago.

'Bob gave me one of your business cards, though, and it said Natalie Caravello on it ... ?'

'Nat and I worked together after we left Wow!,' she explained, 'and there was a year here at the show where I'd forgotten my cards and had to use hers.'

For the tenth time that day, Jamie asked himself just how he could have got it all so wrong.

They had talked for hours in the coffee shop, until close to five o'clock, when both needed to make a move back to their respective stands as they would have been missed. Jamie invited her to join them for their company meal at the Temple, and she had been delighted to accept.

Snapped back to the present, Jamie looked at his watch; it was 7:10. He hadn't seen her for over two hours and was missing her already, but more importantly, she was late. Was she not going to show? He felt the butterflies again in his stomach and thought his peripheral vision had changed.

Then he saw her. She walked in the door, immediately caught his eye and waved. Feeling an overwhelming sense of relief, Jamie stood up and beckoned her over. To his surprise, as she approached the table Emily got up and gave her a hug. They seemed to exchange a few words, before Josh also gave her a kiss on the cheek.

'How do you guys know each other?' Jamie had to ask.

'Sammy's my godmother,' Emily replied simply, 'and Josh knows her from family parties, and events he's been to with me organised by the foundation.'

To further add to the strange situation unfolding in front of him, both Bob and Chilly got to their feet on seeing Sam walk in and greeted her warmly.

'Hello, my dear,' said Bob, 'what a lovely surprise!'

'Pleased to see you again,' said Chilly. Of course—there had been some interaction over the brochures, but Jamie hadn't paid much attention as it had been during his darker years.

Sam gave Emily another hug from behind before moving round to sit next to Jamie, giving him a kiss and squeezing his hand. Jamie took the opportunity to look down at her left hand—no sign of a ring. He leaned in to kiss her cheek just as she turned her head towards him, and their lips met.

The whole table fell momentarily silent before a big cheer went up, and Jamie could hear Chilly making whooping noises. Sam and Jamie looked at each other; their eyes locked and both started to laugh. Jamie turned to face the gathered group around the table.

'I'd like you all to meet ...,' he paused, choosing his words. 'I'd like you all to meet Sam.'

ABOUT THE AUTHOR:

JM Hampshire is an English-born fiction author with a fascination for unfortunate incidents, bad timing and awkward situations (either his own or, preferably, other people's). Educated in England, grown in Asia, and matured in Australia, JM's head is full of 'what if ...' scenarios, developed largely as a foil for his own tangled situations and sometimes unfortunate luck. His understated British sense of humour, colourful life experiences and sharp eye for character observation create warm, engaging stories that are funny, real and relatable.

Having lived and worked on four continents, JM has a rich source of ideas and inspiration harvested from his experiences as an engineer, business owner, graphic designer, photographer, salesman, family man, expat and traveller.

JM is now very happily settled in Australia, with his family and dogs. He has been quietly writing fiction for over twenty years and only decided to write seriously when his wife found out, and happened upon some of his work.

COMING SOON

THIS TIME LAST YEAR

What happens at FaB-Ex stays at FaB-Ex

Don Caravello was going along very nicely, thank you. He had a girlfriend, and now he had a job – a job with prospects, and a job which allowed him to admire from afar the enigmatic AJ. Was she a goddess, a disco queen, or simply a girl with attitude from the rough side of Kirkby?

Surprisingly, Don also still had both his testicles, despite the efforts of his girlfriend's older brother, Stiff.

This time last year tells the tangled back story to *Same time next year?* Don Caravello's tragic tale unfolds, his love for a good woman complicated by a teenage crush that has hit him ten years too late.

Under the roof of the annual FaB-Ex exhibition, Don finds his way with the help of the Wow! girls and the team at Haywood's, and in spite of the efforts of Bradley Copchase, his strange son Wallace, and the recurring and unwelcome attentions of Stiff and his gang of cronies.

ISBN 978-0-6454399-0-8